Lone Star Glory

Continuing the Entertaining and Mostly If Not
Always True Adventures of Texas Ranger Jim
Reade and his Blood Brother
Delaware Scout Toby Shaw
in the Time of the Republic of Texas

A Diversion by

Celia Hayes

Watercress Press
San Antonio, 2017

Copyrighted 2017

ALL RIGHTS RESERVED. No part of this book may be reproduced in any form without the written permission for the author, except for brief passages included in brief passages included in research papers, books, newspapers or magazines

A *Watercress Press* book
from Geron & Associates
www. watercresspress.com

ISBN-13: 978-0-9897821-3-5
ISBN-10: 0-9897821-3-1
Cover design by 3iii's Graphic Studios

A Note, with Acknowledgments, and Dedication

As noted in the notes to the first installation of the adventures of Texas Ranger Jim Reade and Delaware (Lenni-Lenape) Indian guide Toby Shaw began as a discussion of a movie remake of a classic and well-loved western serial adventure. It has taken about a year more than I thought to come up with another set of adventures for Jim and Toby, in the days of the Republic of Texas, for which I apologize. The readers of the first set of adventures have waited patiently – and are rewarded at last. I should note that the short adventures in both *Lone Star Sons* and *Lone Star Glory* do not follow a strict chronological time-line – although the first two adventures in *Sons*, and the last adventure in *Glory* are the first and the last, taking place respectively late in 1842 and early in 1849. All the other adventures in both collections fall in somewhere between those two dates. The introduction and reappearance of such characters as Albert Biddle, Jim Reade's parents and family, Lions the white Comanche, and the English spy, Vibart-Jones hints at a logical sequence.

Finally, this book is dedicated to the memory of two gone before me: my father, Page Hayden, and my late business partner, Alice Geron of Watercress Press. I continue with fond memories of their affection and support.

Celia Hayes
September 2017

Contents

1 – Miss Almira Vanishes
The First Adventure

Wherein Jim Reade and Toby Shaw look into
the matter of a missing sweetheart

"It was just in the latest edition of the *Telegraph*!" Jack exclaimed, as the door of the small house which served as home and headquarters for himself, and such of his Rangers quartered in San Antonio. "The Mexes are releasing some of the men in Perote; the oldest and the most ill of them, and it looks like your father will be among them!"

"What?" Jim looked up from the hearth fire, tending to a ladle of melted lead while he cast bullets. Jack and Toby, as well as some of the others had been decidedly humorous of late over his ineptitude as a marksman with his pair of patent Colt revolvers. He set aside the bullet mold among a scattering of bright new bullets, still hot to the touch, and snatched that copy of the *Telegraph and Texas Register* from Jack's hands. "Says who – and when?! Where are they sending them … my god, I must write to my mother!"

"Front page, hoss." Jack replied. "Likely she already knows. It's the doing of the American Consul to Mexico – they done it as a special favor to him. Latest word is that a dozen or so will be sent off on the next American-flagged ship to leave Santa Cruz for Galveston."

"They never should have been sent to that Perote hell-hole," Jim shook out the paper, and held it to the firelight so that he could better read the tight-packed lines of print. "That slimy, two-faced toad Santa Anna should be burning in hell, first for going back on his world after Velasco ... and then for imprisoning free men going about their own business in their own country."

"In good time, hoss – in good time." Jack answered. "Paint me surprised, if that man ever manages to die in bed of old age. My money is on being shot at dawn, or hung by the neck until dead. Still, I'm guessing that you want to head home to Galveston for the happy reunion?"

"Of course, Jack; can you spare me for a couple of weeks?"

"Certain, hoss – a pity that you can't take Mr. Shaw with you and show him that there is more to Texas than just ol' Bexar and the Nueces Strip," Jack allowed. "It's been ... what, three years, you've been working together, as my stiletto-men, guarding each other's backs. You go to Galveston. And if you see anything that requires attention of the official sort on the way or while you are there – sort it out yourself and let me know afterwards."

"Will do, sir," Jim replied, grateful beyond words, even if Jack added, "See if you can get some shooting practice in, hoss, so the time isn't wasted."

"I'll leave tomorrow," Jim made a heroic effort to ignore the teasing over his bad marksmanship with the Colts. There was more to being one of Jacks' chosen stiletto-men than being a gunfighter; it meant using his mind more often than his fists, or anything else in the way of a weapon.

"By the old Camino Arriba, or by packet boat?"

"The old road will be faster and surer than going to Copano and waiting on a boat," Jim replied. "If Mr. Shaw returns from Fort

Belknap earlier than the end of the month, tell him that I will come back that way, and to meet me along the road."

"I will do that," Jack replied, and if he said anything else beyond that, Jim wasn't paying attention. His mind was too firmly fixed on home; that tall white house in Galveston, made even taller by being built on brick pillars, taller than the trees which surrounded it, with open galleries on front and back, open to the fresh salt-sea breezes from the Gulf. There, on the upper floor gallery, he and his father were accustomed to sit of an evening after supper, watching the sun set in a glorious blaze of orange and gold, while the wind rustled the leaves of the palm trees. So much of his education in the law had taken place on those evenings, listening to Pa and having Pa quiz him about his studies in Blackstone's Commentaries.

All of that had come to an abrupt end three years ago. One morning, Pa had a letter from a jubilant client, saying that his case was finally going to be heard at the district court in San Antonio – the first court meeting in a good few years. The senior Mr. Reade gave instructions for management of the household to his wife, and recommendations as to various matters to do with the law practice to Jim, packed a small carpetbag and departed the following morning – not to return until now. The Mexican General Woll and his army made a lightning-fast raid, deep into Texas, and taken San Antonio, capturing nearly every Anglo man of note in the city, including officers of the court, plaintiffs, and their lawyers. The aftermath of that raid saw Jim sworn in as a Ranger in his brother's company ... then Daniel dead by the hand of treachery and Jim taking his dead brother's place as one of Jack Hays' stiletto-men. He had returned to Galveston now and again over those three years, to a sad, quiet house, where Ma and Daniel's wife Rebecca moved through the duties of their days almost lifelessly, as if such tasks were habits they could not put aside. But now Pa was coming home, after three brutal years of captivity in Perote Prison.

Jim kept himself from pushing his horse too hard over the next two weeks, hurrying up the well-traveled road which went east from San Antonio, through the cool dark pine woods around Bastrop, east to Houston and Nacogdoches and beyond toward Louisiana. At Baytown, he took deck passage for himself and his horse on the first available paddle steamer going out toward Galveston. A fresh breeze ruffled the waters of Trinity Bay – a body of water bigger than any lake could be, edged by narrow ribbons of green and low-lying marsh. Why, stand upon a tall chair, and one could see for miles, as if from the tallest mountain! From the upper gallery of the Reade house, one could see for miles out in the Gulf – indeed, one of the Reade's neighbors had built an even taller house, with an observatory on the roof, from which he could watch ships coming into port through a telescope.

The paddle-wheel steamer fussed it's across Galveston Bay and into port, bobbing like a June-bug in a heavy breeze. It was mid-morning, and the port a scene of a lively bustle, both in the anchorage and along the wharf. Among those ships tied up along the wharf was a Yankee clipper whose three masts towered over the docks. It appeared as if they were making ready to sail; white canvas sails blossomed from her yardarms, and the chanting of sailors as they hauled in the gangplank floated on the air like music. The clipper was a magnificent spectacle – one of the largest ships which Jim had ever seen, and he wondered if she was truly as fast as she was beautiful. No time to stop and watch as she laid on every acre of canvas … he was in a hurry to be home. He crossed the Strand,

4

past the building housing the office which had been his father's place of business. How soon would Pa wish to reopen his practice, and would he wish Jim to set aside his Ranger duties and return to the practice of law? Jim decided not to think about that.

His parents' house and the garden surrounding it looked much as it always had; a tall, white-pillared house, set about with a scattering of spindly trees, and a half-dozen palm trees, which to him always looked more like an up-ended feather duster than a proper tree. Water for a garden was always short in Galveston, dependent on rain, and plagued by the salt in the air; but the rose bushes so cherished by his mother were in vigorous bloom. A few toys were scattered on the lower gallery; balls, hoops, tops and the like. A hobby horse lay abandoned on the area of raked gravel and green weeds which his mother had tried to cultivate into a greensward. Yes – this had always been a happy home, even in the early days, when he and Daniel and his sisters were children. It looked like Daniel and Rebecca's two boys and their little sister had been allowed indulgent rein.

Jim rode around to the stable and the summer-kitchen at the back of the house, and put up his horse in an empty stall. The stable was empty; only a stray chicken wandering in to pick at the corn scattered among the straw. He took his bag and walked toward the back of the house, just as Fat Nella emerged from the summer-kitchen, a tray in her hands. Fat Nella was not really fat, but as tall and strong as a man, sturdy and capable, a free woman of color but hardly darker than Toby Shaw, who was full-blood Delaware. Fat Nella's husband, Big John, was also free, but dark and wiry, nearly pure African. Jim's mother was a Yankee from New England, and

of Abolitionist sympathies – about which the Reade family kept a
tactful silence. They kept no slaves, only freedmen and women to
work in their household for board and regular wages.

"Mistah James! You home just in time! I made up dis supper
tray for Massah Reed! Oh, my lord, he look so poorly! What did
they do to him in that awful Perote place!"

"Nothing good, Nella, I am sure. I'll take the tray for Pa." That
was Rebecca's voice, gentle and calm – his sister-in-law, Daniel's
widow. "Welcome home, James. I'll take it up to him, Nella – thank
you for your trouble in fixing the things that Pa-in-law likes best."

"You make certain that he don't eat too much or too fast, Mizz
Rebecca – they starved him for sure in that nasty place!" Nella
handed over to tray to Rebecca and vanished back into the summer-
kitchen, while Rebecca smiled tranquilly at Jim. Daniel's wife was
a grave and handsome woman some years older than Jim, still clad
in black for the death of her husband, but attractive for all that. That
she was still unmarried after three years marked her out as a woman
of principal and devotion, and not one inclined to rush headlong into
the arms of a man promising to be a good provider. There were very
few respectable young women in Texas, and a generous sufficiency
of bold young men.

"Rebecca – how is Pa? Is he well? I came as fast as I could,
once I heard the good news…"

"Very thin, and terribly tired, but well, Brother James." Jim
held open the back door for her, as they crossed the gallery. "He is
likely sleeping. Your mother has been beside herself with joy all
this week; she and Mr. Nichols are in the parlor. You should go to
her now, while I take this up to your father."

"Mr. Nichols?" Jim stopped at the foot of the stairs. "I don't recall a Nichols among our friends or clients – who is this person?"

"Jeremiah Nichols from Bastrop, who was imprisoned with your father, and released with him," Rebecca answered, as she carried the tray up to the first landing. "He was among Captain Dawson's company, and survived the massacre on the Salado. Daniel and I knew his father and brothers well, since they kept a gristmill. Jeremiah not so much, as he had his own place on the other side of Fayette County. He is a very pleasant gentleman," Rebecca added, as she vanished with the tray around the turn in the stairs. Jim heard her footfalls on the uncarpeted floor above. The door to the parlor was open, to facilitate the wandering and cooling breeze. He tapped on the doorjamb.

"Anyone at home?" he said, and Mrs. Reade leaped to her feet, scattering her embroidery hoop and a skein of thread at her feet.

"Jemmy! My darling boy – this is such a pleasant surprise, you were not expected for weeks. We wrote to you of course, but …"

"The news of Pa's release was in the newspapers," Jim embraced his mother. "I was in Bexar for once, not out on patrol. Jack gave leave at once and I came as swiftly as I could."

"Your father will be so pleased," Mrs. Reade sniffed. "Oh, my – I am convinced that you have grown taller, since you were home last." She reached up – for Emily Reade was a small, and comfortably plump woman, and cupped his face in her hands. "I can never get over how much you have grown, how much you look like Daniel! Our dear Daniel – but Rebecca has been such a help these last few years; our daughter by marriage, even more dear than blood."

"I'm to go up to Pa, as soon as he is properly awake, Rebecca says," Jim made his voice sound steady and bracing. "She said I was to be introduced to Mr. Nichols."

"Don't trouble yourself, Mrs. Reade," replied the gentleman who rose from the settee as soon as Mrs. Reade had started from her chair. "Jeremiah Nichols, at your service, sir. You must be James. Your mother has been regaling me with stories of your service as a Ranger."

Jeremiah Nichols was a lanky man of about thirty, dark-haired and pale from long confinement. His clothing hung on his frame as if on a scarecrow. Jim shook his hand, seeing how his fingers were callused and scarred, and his wrists were also scarred with galls. The Texians taken captive in San Antonio and taken after the Salado Creek fight had been put in chains, and often kept in them for punishment.

"Ma does exaggerate, but I am pleased to make the acquaintance of any man who was my father's fellow in captivity," Jim said. Jeremiah Nichols grinned in reply. "The pleasure is wholly mine, sir! Any son of Elisha Reade, Esquire, is instantly a friend indeed. I hear that you are one of Captain Hays' company in Bexar and that is a high recommendation indeed."

"Among my duties and responsibilities," Jim replied. "Rebecca says that your family is settled in Bastrop, and well-acquainted with my brother. Are you intending to remain in Galveston long?"

"For a few days, whilst I regain my land legs and become accustomed to breathing the free air again," Jeremiah Nichols sank back onto the settee with a small apology. "I suffered from the ague and other ailments during these last few months. My life was despaired of by the doctor who was imprisoned with us, so that is why I was released. I expect the Mexes didn't think I would live for much longer anyway, but they underestimated how revivifying freedom would be, after three years in Perote."

"If you intend returning to Bastrop, then we may travel together," Jim offered. "Captain Hays has allowed me several weeks leave with my family, before he requires my return. I will be traveling on the old Spanish Camino. If you can procure a horse for yourself, I'd be glad of the company."

"Thank you, Jim, I would welcome a companion on the journey very much. I long to return home, and would have set out yesterday," Jeremiah Nichols fetched up and long sigh. "But while the spirit may be willing, the flesh is weak, and so I am delayed while I recover. There is a young woman whom I had an understanding with, before I went with Dawson. I had a single letter from her early in my imprisonment. Miss Almira Clark promised that she would wait for me, but in two years since then I have not received another letter."

"I am certain that your young lady kept to her word," Mrs. Reade insisted, with an air of robust cheer, just as Rebecca appeared in the doorway.

"Papa Reade is ready to see you now, James," she said, "He is on the upper gallery, in his favorite chair."

Jim hastily excused himself from the parlor and took the familiar stairs two at a time. Daniel may have been the oldest son, but he knew that he had been most particularly cherished by his father for having similar tastes and temperament. Then there was the practice of law, in which Daniel had never taken any interest to speak of.

Elisha Reade reclined on a willow-work chaise set out on the upper gallery – the same one which he was accustomed to sit with Jim in the old days. He had a dressing gown on over his shirt, and a light robe laid over his lap in the manner of an invalid; Jim's heart contracted in his chest. Pa's whiskers had grown in entirely gray. He looked twenty years older, withered and grown smaller, although he had formerly been a vigorous and fine-appearing man. He had the same vivid galls on his wrists – the scars of chains and shackles, and he was thin … so thin!

"H'lo, Pa," Jim said, hesitating in the door to the upper gallery. "I'm home – dear god, Pa – don't get up."

"I'm fine," Elisha Read insisted, making an attempt to disentangle his legs from the robe. "No, maybe not," he admitted with a sigh. He sank back upon the wicker chaise, and Jim bent over him for a fine and fatherly embrace. "I will blame it on your mothers' attempts to make pies and invalid puddings for me. The dearest of womanhood to me, but she cannot cook and bake. Rebecca and Fat Nella gently conspire to save me from the worst of it … James, I had expected to find you here, when I returned! Yet they will tell me that you were in Bexar and for most of the past three years, so your mother assured me. No one would tell me why or what you were doing!"

"They did not know," Jim admitted. He pulled up one of the straight chairs and sat upon it. The tray which Rebecca had brought up sat upon a folding stand, the covered dishes on it so far untouched. "You should eat, Pa – you look as if you have been starved."

"Well, yes, I have been," Elisha Read admitted. Jim uncovered the largest dish, and handed his father the fork which had been set beside it.

"Then, Pa – a bite of your dinner for every question answered. The first answer is a bonus, to tease your appetite. I have been in Bexar … well, mostly in Bexar, ever since you were taken. I … well, Daniel swore me into his company after the Salado Creek fight. We both went with Captain Hays and General Somervell's army, chasing after Woll. We were all supposed to try and rescue you and the others, before Woll and his army crossed over into Mexico. But before that happened…" Jim's throat closed, part in the memory of that grief and for what he had not been able to say until now. "I couldn't tell you any more about that, Pa – not while you were a prisoner in Perote. Who knew who would be reading my letters before you received them. I could not say anything other than that Daniel was dead, murdered by a parcel of renegades. I took service then with Captain Hays, to pursue Daniel's murderers, and serve the nation of Texas the best that I could. That's where I have been, all these three years – not drawing up writs and wills, and waiting for the next court to assemble. I am sorry, Pa – I'm afraid that our practice has gone into something like arrears, these past few years…"

"Never mind, Jim," Elisha Reade patted Jim's knee. "You were doing good service, son. And I am proud. Yes, indeed – I am proud. Fit to bursting my buttons proud…"

"I can't tell you of much of it, Pa," Jim confessed. "Most of it was matters of state, and of the rest … matters that I cannot talk of. But all of it was useful, and in pursuit of justice and law. And not all that dangerous. Well, in bits and pieces, sometimes. I have been mostly entangled in resolving feuds and mysteries."

"Your brother would be proud, too!" Elisha Reade began eating, small and careful bites, which Jim watched anxiously. "Your mother does not know the details, I assume? I would not want her to worry."

"I will not say very much other to Ma than I have the trust of reliable allies and even that of the Penateka Comanche, through one of their most respected chiefs. We are friends with Mopechucope, Old Owl they call him. My most stalwart comrade is another Indian; Toby Shaw of the Delaware, the nephew of their chief, Jim Shaw. He is visiting his family, or he would have come to Galveston with me. I cannot say how glad I am that you have been released, Pa."

"Glad about that myself," Elisha Reade returned, with a sigh. "My only regret is that more of us poor prisoners were not freed with us. But there is talk abroad of an armistice agreement between Texas and Mexico – which, once signed, will mean that the remainder of those imprisoned in that foul place will be released unconditionally. Still, my conscience sometimes pricks me; I should have refused parole and remained in solidarity. My words and actions sometimes served to … defuse certain situations when the more reckless among us clashed with our guards. I am afraid that without my guidance … certain hotheads may provoke a dangerous encounter."

"Water under the bridge, Pa," Jim eyed the food on his father's plate, which was diminishing in careful bites. "By the look of you – and of Mr. Nichols, as well – you couldn't have lasted there much longer. We're glad enough to have you home, and so will Mr. Nichol's young lady in Bastrop be glad of his return."

"True enough." Elisha Read admitted. He scraped up the last few bites on the largest plate, and regarded the smaller plate on which a slice of buttermilk pie rested. "Dare I hope that Nella made the pie, and not your mother? The most admirable of wives, but my dear lady cannot set foot in a kitchen without incurring a disaster. When we first married, our most urgent need was the hire of a cook – we would have starved otherwise."

"Allow me, Pa." Jim picked up the unused spoon from the tray, slivered off the narrowest corner of the pie, and tasted it carefully. "Definitely Nella's making. Don't worry – I'll have a slice of my own, later."

"You do that, son." Elisha Reade already looked tired again, as if eating a light meal was almost too much of an effort. "I'm almost recovered, I promise you. This evening … come up and sit with me, as you used to do. I shall need to begin recovering my practice again. If you are at liberty for the next few weeks, may I ask you to run errands … reopen the office. It would be of such help to me, and keep yourself occupied."

"Certainly, Pa." Jim promised. "You won't have to lift a finger – just recover your health."

"I will, most certainly – now that I am home." Elisha Reade promised.

Over the following fortnight, Jim immersed himself in a comfortable home-life routine that he had nearly forgotten; eating regular and varied meals, expertly cooked by Fat Nella, sleeping in an upstairs room, set with tall windows, and filmy curtains stirring mist-like in the night breezes which blew off the Gulf. He slept on a proper bed – not on a pallet laid out on a crude wooden frame strung with rawhide strips in a windowless inner room in the adobe house that was Jack's headquarters in Bexar. To his joy and relief, his father improved in strength and color every day, reviving like a cut plant placed in a pitcher of water. Jeremiah Nichols improved likewise, although his clothing still hung on him like a scarecrow. Within days, he was helping Jim to reopen the offices of Reade & Reade, Atty's at Law – which offices had been closed up for three years, and such valuable furniture and trunks of records conveyed for safekeeping to the Reade house. He grew to like Jeremiah Nichols, who as he recovered his own strength revealed a rather dry sense of humor, which accorded very well with Jim and an interest in things to do with public matters. Nichols read the *Telegraph and Texas Register*, and those other newspapers which arrived at the Reade household with deep attention and interest, and discussed those matters contained in them with anyone who could not escape fast enough.

"My father says that you should study law," Jim suggested on a morning some ten days following his arrival in Galveston. "You have an interest in public matters, and a sense of logic. He says that you would do very well – if it is a calling you wish to pursue. You might yet do very well at it, if I am any judge."

"I might, at that," Jeremiah Nichols replied. They were walking back from the row of frame buildings in the business part of town which housed Reade & Reade. "But I must first return to Bastrop – to my dear Almira … Miss Clarke, that is. It is a matter of distress that I have never had any answers to my letters. I wrote to her, upon my arrival here – saying that I lived, and would return to her as soon as the condition of my health permitted … and even then, I have now answer. I know from my friends that her family still is established at Bastrop … but I think that if something about their situation had changed, if they had removed from Texas entirely – I would know of it. I think of her often. She has a most engaging smile. A rather plain girl, but when she smiled – enchanting. It is a distressing puzzle, Mr. Reade, that I have not heard from her, or from her family."

"Call me Jim, if I may be on terms so familiar as to call you Jeremiah," Jim suggested.

Jeremiah grinned. "We may as well, since I suppose that we are to be companions when I return to Bastrop."

"Then, if I accompany you throughout your journey," Jim suggested. "And there such a mystery regarding your beloved – permit me the opportunity to unravel it. I'm very good at unraveling mysteries of this kind," he added. "I think that I may have prevented a particularly vexing feud between two families, through solving the question of a vanishing lady, some years ago…"

"Where had this lady gone?" Jeremiah asked, as they turned into the walkway leading through the Reade's garden.

"She had run away to marry another suiter," Jim replied. "One not favored by her family. I thought it a very sensible decision on her own part," he added, as they climbed the stairs to the first floor. "The feud had the potential to become particularly deadly. The two families were at loggers' heads until Mr. Shaw and I deduced where she had gone and intervened."

"I do not think that Almira would have played so false with me, as to run away with another," Jeremiah mused. "She was of a tender and devoted temperament … not the sort of woman to play suiters against each other … Mrs. Reade – I implore your pardon, I did not see you."

"I contrive to melt into the background," Rebecca answered, with some amusement. "In the way of a widow, plagued with suiters. If I had a loom, I would weave on it constantly, and unravel the work by night, like Penelope, the wife of Odysseys. How goes the work of establishing Pa-in-law's practice? I am so happy that both of you are willing to devote yourselves to the work of restoring it! Pa-in-law has received so many callers over the last few days – as many as were old friends wishing to assure themselves of his good health, there were twice again hoping that he would soon renew his practice and they could avail themselves of his service."

"Pa may have been modest in speaking of it," Jim explained to Jeremiah, who seemed to be a trifle taken back by Rebecca's words, although he did smile at the allusion. "But he is one of the best-respected lawyers in this part of Texas. I think that returning to that work may be the best tonic of all. I do not expect to linger for much longer in Galveston, once I am certain that my father is back in the traces. Are you also recovered, enough for a horseback journey, Jeremiah?"

"I do believe that I am," that gentleman replied. "The absence of word from Miss Clarke concerns me … although I will miss the splendid company and hospitable care from Mrs. Reade, the elder and Mrs. Reade the younger."

Jim did note that Rebecca pinkened slightly; she and Jeremiah were amiable, easy company with each other. But for the ghost of Daniel, and Jeremiah's fondness for that Miss Almira Clarke of Bastrop, he would have thought they were at the beginning of a gentle flirtation with each other.

"I think that we must begin our journey next week," Jim said – he had been better than three weeks in Galveston, and leisure was beginning to make him more restless than he was reluctant to admit. No, now that Pa was free, and well-traveled on the road to recovery, Jim was as bored and as jumpy as a boy confined in a schoolroom on a hot spring day. "How soon can you hire yourself a good horse?"

***

In the end, Jim and his father had to purchase the horse, for it seemed that Jeremiah had nothing more in his pockets than the lint at the bottom of them. Of his property in Fayette County, there would have been no income without him to work at it.

"He's an enterprising young man, he'll return the cost of hire with interest," Elisha Reade confidently assured Jim on the evening before their departure. "I am content to wait. Perhaps the government will make some kind of settlement on us former prisoners."

"Altogether likely that settlement will be in the form of land certificates," Jim pointed out. "Land is all that the Republic has. As near as can be told, the treasury is bare of anything else. We even had to rent out the ships of our Navy to the rebels of the Yucatan."

"Sufficient unto the day," his father exclaimed, jaunty as ever. "In the meantime, son, I devote myself to my old practice, and grateful to be able to do so. It has been a joy to have you home again, even if just for a short time. I will confess that I will miss your keen eyes and neat hand at writing out writs and petitions ... but you have answered a higher calling. Do be careful on your journey back to Bexar, and in your duties once you return to them. And remember to write to your mother and I as often as you can."

"I will, Pa," Jim promised, slightly regretting the necessity of returning, but the duties of a Ranger, like that of a careful housewife, were never done.

He and Jeremiah took a gentle pace when they set out from Baytown, meandering west by easy stages, sometimes in company with other travelers but more often just the two of them. They spent most nights sleeping in the open, unrolling their blankets under a sheltering tree, watching the stars silently wheeling overhead. The weather was mild, for spring was just coming on, the fields and meadows thick with flowers, the tree leaves coming out in delicate, yellow-green leaves. Other evenings, when the clouds promised rain, they took hospitality at farmsteads, or at taverns and boarding establishments. Very often, when their hosts learned that Jeremiah was a newly-freed Perote prisoner, such hospitality was offered with open-handed generosity. Jeremiah talked often of Almira Clark, of her many fine qualities and of their courtship. He did not mention his worry about not hearing from her, all the time he was in Perote more often than once or twice a day.

"I suppose that we should go to the mill, first," Jeremiah allowed, on the day that they came over the last thick-wooded hill, and could see the scattered roofs of Bastrop below, with the dark blue-green waters of the Colorado etched into the landscape beyond. There was a ford through the shallows, where the old road dropped over a gentle bank and out of sight.

"Your folks will be expecting you," Jim said, by way of encouragement. His own heart lifted at the sight of familiar face. Toby Shaw sat before a simple shelter around the next bend, a small brush arbor built against a massive fallen tree by the side of the

Camino. Toby got to his feet unhurriedly and lifted his hand in greeting.

"You took your time, Brother," he remarked. "I have been waiting for you here, these past three days. Captain Jack assured me you would be traveling by this road."

"Sorry to have kept you," Jim grinned and performed the introductions. "Mr. Nichols is of this town, and has a family and sweetheart waiting for him, but we could not hurry on any faster than we did. Where's your horse?"

"I walked," Toby picked up his war club, his blanket, already neatly rolled and the skin bag which formed his only baggage. "A man travels swiftly when he travels with the least." He fell into an easy-ground covering jog, a pace which Jim knew from experience would match a horse at any pace but a dead gallop and which Toby could maintain without ever becoming notably out of wind.

"Where is this mill of yours?" Jim asked, as they passed the first of the scattered houses and buildings. There were few people about on this afternoon, a day when all had business to attend.

"About a quarter mile north, along the river. We dug out a good deep millrace, the first year that we settled. As long as there is water in the river, my brothers keep the mill-wheel turning."

Bastrop was a long-settled town, as things in Texas went, but still not very long, compared to Bexar, La Bahia or Natchitoches. Just long enough to have had a Spanish garrison for a time, but nothing as notable and permanent as a mission or a presidio. But the scattering of streets were wide and lined with timber and stone buildings in the style of the American settlers. Just as they passed by the largest – a general store by the look of the place – a young man emerged from the door, and as his eyes adjusted to the daylight, he exclaimed,

"My god, Jeremiah, is it really you? We all heard that you were dead – that the Mexes executed you at Saltillo for attempting to escape! We thought it was all true, so help me!"

"Reuben Wilcox! As I live and breathe, so I tell you it is not true. I drew a white bean, and spent two years in Perote for my trouble. Tell me – is Almira Clarke still waiting for me? Tell me true, for I have not heard a word from her, since a letter I received months after Salado. She promised that she would wait for me..."

"I am sure that she has waited," Reuben Wilcox replied, seeming honest and open, but something in Jim's lawyerly experience alerted him to a brief hesitation as he answered, a certain evasive expression. Honest men answered straight and so did practiced liars, but in Jim's experience *(bolstered by his fathers')* men and women too, on the spot and considering a lie always displayed that small hesitation. There was a sort of fleeting, calculating expression on their face, which Elisha Reade insisted was a dead giveaway that a lie was about to be told.

"Let us proceed to your brother's place of business," Jim urged, and Jeremiah nodded absently as Reuben Wilcox bade them farewell.

"The Clarke's have a place to the south of Bastrop," Jeremiah said. "Ru Wilcox is their nearest neighbor. I will go calling on them tomorrow. Would you accept our hospitality for the night, or for as long as you wish to linger before returning to Bexar? I feel that I owe you a return for the kindness of your family in Galveston."

"Of course," Jim replied. "I wish to meet the excellent Miss Clarke, after listening to you describe her many fine qualities."

"Excellent," Jeremiah beamed, although a shadow returned to his face as they followed the road that ran in a northerly direction from Bastrop, a road well-established by the passage of many wagons.

"Business must have been well, for the gristmill," Jim commented. Jeremiah nodded in agreement. "It seems at once an age since I came this way, and yet at the same time, only a day or so ago. Have you ever had that feeling, Jim?"

"Now and again," was all that Jim could say, for at that moment, the track dipped down toward the river, and they could see the gristmill, with the ceaselessly turning wheel, water droplets sparkling in the sun as they fell off the bottom of the paddle-wheel. The constant growl of millstones turning rose slightly above the splashing water.

"I never thought I would see this again," Jeremiah said, very softly to Jim. There were several wagons standing in the mill-yard; customers bringing last year's harvest of corn and wheat to be ground into flour. "There were nights when I dreamed of this place ... and then when I woke, in a stone cell in Perote, I would come close to weeping, Most unmanly ..."

A man came out of the mill, carrying a full sack of flour over each shoulder, catching sight of them as he tipped one bag and then the other into the closest wagon.

"Jeremiah!" he shouted, and came at a run. "Hey, Pa! Lige! Jeremiah's home!"

This must be one of the brothers; the same build and coloring. Exuberant with welcome, he all but pulled Jeremiah off his horse, roughly embracing and then pounding his shoulders, until Jeremiah begged for mercy, and two more men appeared from the mill. Jim and Toby stood a little aside, not wanting to impose on a joyous family reunion. At last, though, Jeremiah begged for mercy again, and introduced them to his brothers, Nathaniel and Elijah, and their father Daniel.

"You will see that Ma is a very devout woman," Jeremiah added, and all three of the Nichols men grinned. "You'll stay with us, of course – Ma wouldn't hear of anything else. I guess you'll have to settle with me for a supper of fatted calf."

"I wouldn't accept anything less," Jim grinned, recalling how Fat Nella, his mother and Rebecca conspired to spoil his father by preparing those dishes that were his favorites.

The Nichols house was part of the mill and stables complex; a sprawling dog-trot cabin with additions, to which they were made welcome. Mrs. Nichols was a bossy little banty-hen of a woman, completely in charge of her household. Jim and his blood-brother were given the use of the best extra room. The only unsettling moment came when Jeremiah mentioned Miss Clarke to his mother.

"I thought I'd ride over to the Clarke place tomorrow," he said, with an air of elaborate unconcern. "And pay my respects to Almira. Were you able to tell her of my release from Perote, Ma?"

"I haven't seen Almira in some long time," Mrs. Nichols admitted. "I understand that she has been quite poorly since you been gone."

"That's right," brother Nathaniel admitted, and his mother chided him for speaking with his mouth full. Nathaniel swallowed, adding, "She didn't come to that Methodist camp-meeting last spring. That was some powerful preaching and testifying. Them Clarke menfolk were at that camp meeting, too, all but Miss Almira and her mother. I reckon everyone in the county was there, weren't they, Ma?"

"Indeed, they were," Mrs. Nichols nodded. "But recollect, Mary was one of those Papists from San Patricio way afore she married Jabez Clarke. I thought at the time … it was just because Almira was said to be feeling mighty low, but that preaching would have roused Lazarus from his deathbed."

"Here," Jeremiah asked in sudden alarm. "Almira hasn't gone courting some other fellow after she promised to wait for me? I'd purely understand if she had broken her word and everyone feared to tell me of it. She hasn't married some other spark, has she?"

"Ru Wilcox was pretty keen on her," Elijah Nichols mumbled into his plate, until told to hush by his mother.

"Nothing of the sort," Mrs. Nichols clicked her tongue disparagingly and shook her head over the careless ways of flibbertigibbet young girls these days. "I was speaking to Mary just after Christmas last and she said they were piecing a double-wedding-ring quilt for her, in anticipation of you and her marrying."

The moment passed without further comment, although Jim did note in passing that Jeremiah looked momentarily cast down. That Miss Almira Clarke and her mother were absent from one of an enormous camp meeting … even if one wasn't particularly enthralled with Methodist teachings, a camp meeting would have been an excuse for one of the largest social gatherings in the county. Jim feared that on the morrow, Jeremiah would discover that his dear and cherished Miss Almira had become a hopeless invalid. Taking to ones' bed with a case of consumption, or some other wasting illness would have been the only reason for such an absence. And perhaps her family was in two minds over how to break the news of this to Jeremiah.

On the following morning, the Nichols family and their guests breakfasted in the open breezeway of their house, as was the custom of those households in Texas where the days were warm even in winter, assuming there was no blue norther blowing. Mrs. Nichols spoke to Jim of how they had prospered with the gristmill, and hoped to soon build a modern and larger house – because a log dwelling was a poor and primitive thing – a house with proper glass windows, and a deep gallery all the way around. Jeremiah saddled his horse and rode off to his appointment with the Clarkes, and the other menfolk departed to attend to their daily labors in the mill. Jim and Toby, having wordlessly agreed to travel on as soon as hospitality permitted, were stayed by Mrs. Nichols.

Out of the blue, she said, as she came from the kitchen part of the house, "You should remain here with us, Mr. Reade. At least until Jeremiah returns from the Clarkes."

"And why should we impose on your generous hospitality any farther?" Jim was prepared to be indulgent, for the Nichols family had been especially accommodating to his blood-brother, treating him simply as a welcome guest, without further comment.

"There's something queer going on with those Clarkes, and our Jeremiah's intended." Mrs. Nichols admitted honestly, which Jim appreciated, since it was about the first time that someone had baldly stated the case. "Almira is a good girl, fit and proper for a wife to one of my sons. Nichols and I couldn't have picked a better wife for him, I'm telling you honest and straight. But she hasn't been seen since about mid-summer last year. And that is a worrisome thing."

Mrs. Nichols paused in her clearing away the breakfast plates, and the empty serving dishes. "They – them Clarkes – they live a fair piece from town, so it is not as if they are folk that we see, often in the ordinary way of things – mebbe at a bee or a roof-raising, which isn't often. I think it is right peculiar that a pretty young girl can suddenly vanish this way. Her family and kin insist that all is well ... but there is still something wrong, when it comes to her and our Jeremiah. I'm not a fanciful sort," and Mrs. Nichols gathered up the last of the dirty dishes, "But there is something curious with that. And Jeremiah will either find it out, or return with more questions. Everyone says that you two," and her glance encompassed Toby as well, "Are good at getting answers to hard questions. I did hear some talk that Reuben Wilcox took a shine to her, and thought he might have better luck in his courting after Jeremiah went with Captain Dawson. Not that he had a chance, seeing as how Almira Clarke had eyes for no one other than my Jeremiah."

"If it would truly present no trouble for you," Jim sighed, for he truly wanted to resume the journey, "We will linger under your roof for a day or two longer. Your son was a true comrade with my father in Perote. And my father would want me to do whatever is within my power to assist any friend of his."

"Thank you kindly, Mr. Reade – it will be no trouble at all. I've a houseful of men, two more to the number is hardly any trouble to speak of."

"So, what do you think?" Jim asked his blood-brother, when they had the breezeway to themselves. They had obligingly made themselves of use, carrying buckets of water dipped from the millstream for Mrs. Nichols to wash dishes in, and idly discussed whether they should venture along the riverbank hunting game birds or perhaps a good place to fish; fresh fish or waterfowl would be a welcome addition to Mrs. Nichol's pantry, as well as graciously compensating her for setting two more places at her table.

"About this Miss Clarke?" Toby, self-assured and as handsome as any Indian prince in a Deerslayer novel, had a great deal more experience with the fair sex than Jim did, to the point where Jack had often described him as the ladies' delight of at least three nations. "I do not know, James, but it has entered my mind that Jeremiah may have fixed his affections on a dream-woman. The real woman likely has fallen in love with another, and she is too proud, or too embarrassed to speak honestly to him of it."

"That may be true, of course. But marriage was spoken of by her family, though," Jim mused. "Or so Mrs. Nichols said, just about the time of the camp meeting, I think. But this is the other thing; the camp meeting was important. Everyone goes to them, less'n they are dying. Especially young folks, looking to see their friends, do a bit of flirting between the hymn-singing, even a young lady with an understanding. See, and if she was ill, sick in bed, not able to come to the camp meeting – why, everyone would know. They'd have prayers for her, folk would send her their good wishes, come calling with remedies and advice. And if she had died of such … well, everyone would know. There are no secrets when it comes to weddings and funerals. But there's been nothing; the silence on the matter is curious, Brother. We can trust the good Mrs. Nichols' word on that – if she thinks there is something strange going on … well, the older ladies always know."

"So also do they among my people," Toby nodded in glum agreement. "The mothers always know ... sometimes even before their sons and daughters realize. This vanishing of Miss Clarke from the gatherings that your people prize is a significant thing. I do not think that Mr. Nichols will have any good result from his visit to her family."

And no, he had not. Jim and Toby returned from an afternoon spent venturing along the relatively unsettled stretches of the Colorado above Bastrop bearing with them several brace of fat ducks, and a string of equally fat trout, to find Jeremiah sitting in the breezeway, distressed and defeated from his long-anticipated visit to the home of his beloved.

"I don't understand it," he said, for the sixth or seventh time. "They told me that she was gone. And they wouldn't say why, or with whom. And without leaving any word to me! That's the part that I cannot understand or countenance, fellows. We were pledged to marry, as soon as the traveling preacher could wed us together in those sacred bonds. I had that in her single letter to me! If she had chosen another, in my absence; that I could understand, however painful that intelligence would be to me. But she would have communicated that to me – come to me or conveyed it, written in a letter. There is something wrong about this," and he looked at Jim with such and honest expression, filled with pain and misery. "We loved each other, dear and true – not just as sweethearts, but also as friends, having known each other since in small-clothes."

"Your mother thinks that there is some puzzle that we can solve," Jim admitted. "It just isn't you, wondering what has become of Miss Almira Clark. My brother here is a man of considerable experience with the fair ladies of his nation; he also thinks there is something amiss. Captain Hays gave me wide latitude when he gave me leave to visit my family, saying that if anything struck me as being a matter of taking an official interest ... that's what Mr. Shaw and I are tasked to do; find people, solve mysteries, protect the interests of our citizens and our nation. A woman missing is definitely within that range. Do you want us to see what we can find out about your sweetheart?"

"Yes," Nathanial gave a decided nod. "If it would not cause you any more trouble than you have already been put to."

"Then we will do so – to put your mind at ease, and perhaps to spare the feelings of a lady. But once we are on the path of finding the truth of what has happened to Miss Clarke, will you promise to accept whatever facts that we find? That if she has married another, you will not bear a grudge, or raise a challenge? It is not in ours or anyones' interest to set off another deadly feud, you know."

"I do so," Jeremiah promised readily. "And you may have a chance to talk to Almira's young brother in two or three days. Dan Clarke said that young Dan would be bringing a wagonload of corn to be milled this week."

"Good," Jim thought about the means of carrying out this investigation without stepping on any sensitive toes. "Then Mr. Shaw and I will go hunting tomorrow. We may go farther than we did today. Perhaps in the direction of the Clarke place ... how is the hunting in those parts?"

"Deer sometimes," Jeremiah grinned. "And wild hog, but be careful. Clarke lets his run loose in the woods, and he wouldn't take kindly to someone butchering out one of them. I'll make you a map;

Wilcox's place is a good piece downstream from town, and the Clarkes' just beyond that."

The set out the following morning, after a sumptuous breakfast cooked by Jeremiah's mother. Jim reckoned that was her means of expressing her gratitude for investigating the mysterious, months-long absence of Almira Clarke from such gatherings as women of all ages commonly relished. The Nichols menfolk, to include Jeremiah, had their work in the mill, or in the garden patch to attend – and likely they relished the taste of fresh game or fresh fish, also, since their regular work offered little opportunity to go hunting. Pa Nichols waved to them from the edge of the corn-patch, as Jim and Toby set off on foot, as they had on the previous day; Jim with his rifle, Toby with his bow and quiver of arrows. If they returned with game – all to the better, for the excuse of hunting on a fine spring day was their reason for wandering where they would.

They returned late in the day, as the sun burned red-gold in the western sky, burdened with a tender yearling doe, field-dressed and ready for the butchering. Toby had shot it, neatly and mercifully in the heart, murmuring the customary thanks-and-blessing prayer.

They had already found that thing which might hint at a somber answer to their inquiries, on the hillside above where they had flushed out the young deer. There was a small fenced enclosure, and a short way from it, a narrow mound planted in white flowers – the wild white lilies that always blossomed prodigiously after a good rain.

"There was no marking," Toby had said. "That is contrary to the custom of your people, is it not, James?"

"It is, indeed." Jim looked out from the edge of the thicket; below them was a well-built house of sawn planks rather than crude logs, the center of a small constellation; stable, smokehouse, summer-kitchen, a grain-bin, pens for the tame cattle and horses – all attesting to the success of the Clarke holding on the Colorado, in this world and in the next. "We will see what young Mr. Clarke has to say, when he brings a load of corn to the mill. It might be well to speak with Mr. Wilcox too, if chance puts us in his way."

"Well, what did you find?" Jeremiah demanded upon their return; his clothing powdered with flour from the mill, but his face, hair and hands still damp from a hasty clean-up at the water trough. Jim exchanged a warning glance with his blood-brother.

"Nothing we can say much of without talking to Dan Clarke in private," Jim replied. "We spoke with Mrs. Clarke, to introduce ourselves, and Mr. Clarke, to ask permission to hunt on his land, but we did not say anything about our true purpose. We found ..." Jim hesitated. "We may have some notion about Miss Clarke's whereabouts. But it is a theory, only. More than that, I do not want to say. Not until we can talk with young Clarke."

"As long as you are still looking for answers," Jeremiah sounded glum; Jim and Toby exchanged another meaningful look.

The wagon from the Clarke place came up the track from Bastrop, early the following morning, much to Jim's relief. He didn't relish another day wasted, hanging around the Nichols place, trying to appear as if he and Toby had some serious task to perform.

The wagon was driven by a boy of about eleven or twelve years of age. With him was another man on horseback. As wagon and horseman approached, Jim recognized Reuben Wilcox, who had spoken to Jeremiah outside of the general store; who owned the next property to the Clarkes and courted Almira Clarke, if Mrs. Nichols was correct – and as a sharp-eyed elder woman in a small town, she likely was. Yes, he could already see the hazy outline of events. A few words with Almira's young brother and her family's closest neighbor would confirm what he and Toby suspected.

"I didn't know that you were such good friends with Jeremiah," Reuben Wilcox exclaimed, as he saw Jim and Toby sitting in the breezeway of the Nichols house, while Mrs. Nichols shelled a quantity of fresh-picked garden peas. "I assumed that you were chance companions on the road … take the corn to the mill, lad – time's a wasting."

"In a moment," Jim stayed the boy, as he was about to do so. "You're Dan, aren't you? I've always liked the name. I had an older brother named Daniel. You are the younger brother of Miss Almira? If so we have some questions for you. Come and take a moment to sit with us, and answer some questions. It's permissible; we're friends of the Nichols family and empowered by the State to … ask questions regarding certain matters. Do please sit down, both of you, and answer honestly to my questions."

"You shouldn't say a word to them, Dan!" Reuben Wilcox protested, even as he nodded toward Mrs. Nichols and doffed his hat. "They don't have the right…"

"We have that right when we are asked to determine the whereabouts of a person who seems to be missing," Jim replied, flint-hard and at his most lawyerly. "Miss Almira Clarke was a citizen of this town, this locality – yet she is at present nowhere to be found; no one has seen her in some time, and there is no gossip concerning where she might have gone. Mr. Nichols was affianced to marry her upon his return from captivity in Perote. Having no news from her, or of her, he is understandably distressed, as are his family." He fixed the two of them with a stern glance, and Mrs. Nichols paused in her work, and seemed inclined to rise from where she sat. "But I am of the conviction that you both know where she is. Mrs. Nichols, may I ask you to remain as a witness, and as reassurance to young Daniel that we have no ill-intent toward him."

Mrs. Nichols nodded, and continued with shelling peas; the gentle popping sound of splitting pods remained as a constant background to the conversation, while her eyes seemed not to miss anything.

"I don't have any idea of Miss Clarke's whereabouts!" Reuben Wilcox waxed indignant. "Or why she chose to … chose to go… to go away. And call off your pet savage, while you're at it, Reade!"

"Mr. Shaw is my fellow Ranger," Jim returned, unmoved. "And I think you do know Miss Clarke's whereabouts, Mr. Wilcox; she is buried in that unmarked grave at the top of the hill overlooking the Clarke place, a little apart from the marked graves. I believe you know why she is in that grave."

Reuben Wilcox's countenance abruptly went from flushed red to pale with shock. "I don't have to sit here and listen to your vile accusations!" he blustered. Jim agreed, in his blandest tones. "No, you don't, indeed. But there is a curious matter that I wish to resolve – and I ask that you linger long enough to answer my questions. When we met you in the street outside the general mercantile, the day that we arrived in Bastrop, you said something about hearing that Jeremiah Nichols was dead, executed by the Mexicans at Saltillo; was that a rumor going around just before the camp meeting last year? Mrs. Nichols, can you confirm, if Mr. Wilcox won't?"

"There was such a rumor," Mrs. Nichols answered, distressed and indignant. "And cruel it was, for Letty Lacey told me of it, the very day after we had received a letter from Jeremiah, telling us that he was in Perote, months after those poor men were killed in that vile lottery. The rumor was all over town, Letty said. She had no notion of how it started, but we told everyone of his letter, and squashed that nasty tale flat."

"Oh, I have a notion of who started the rumor, or tried to make an advantage for himself in passing it on," Jim turned his attention to young Dan, looking miserably at his hands. "A very good notion. Daniel, your sister heard that rumor, didn't she? That the man she loved was dead, executed at Saltillo." Dan nodded mutely, still looking at his hands. Jim reminded himself of how very young the boy was – too young to bear the burden of adult tragedy – and made his own voice gentle, understanding. "Dan, what did your sister do, when she heard that Jeremiah Nichols was dead. Speak up, lad – we can barely hear you."

"She bundled up rocks in her apron and walked into the river." The boy answered, without raising his head. "I saw her do it, from a distance. She went under and didn't come up. I went to get Pa, but it was too late."

"She killed herself, then," Jim persisted, while Mrs. Nichols gasped in horror. "A mortal sin, as true Christians have it, especially those raised as Catholics, like your mother. But she couldn't bear living, believing that the man she loved was gone from this world."

"Romantic clap-trap!" Reuben Wilcox rose scraping the chair he sat on a little backward as he settled his hat on his head. "I will hear nothing more of this foolishness! I had nothing to do with spreading that rumor – it was told to me…"

"The guilty flee where none pursue," Jim put on his father's best cross-examining manner and voice. "Did you repeat to Miss Almira the rumor that Jeremiah Nichols was dead?"

"He was," Dan Clarke's voice was barely audible. "She told me so herself, the morning that she walked into the river. He'd paid a call, that very day, saying that she had to know that Jeremiah was dead and she need not go on waiting for him."

"I imagine," Jim ventured, "your sister was distraught at being told her sweetheart was dead."

Dan shook his head. "Nossir. She was very calm – neither crying or carrying on. She was just …matter-of-fact. She said she was going to gather wild plums from the thickets by the river, and I was to tell Ma and not to worry. I went to cut firewood from the grove above the river, and when I looked back, I could see her, walking into the river. It was Ma," Now Dan gulped, as if on the verge of giving way to his own grief. "Ma's notion to say anything at all. Pa agreed with her, to keep the peace. Ma said it was a shame and a disgrace to the family, Almira doing away with herself. We should go on as if Almira had never been, say nothing to no one. We lived out and away from town, you see. Kept to ourselves, mostly. But I think Ma was powerful grieved herself. She and Pa took such pride in Almira an' me. It was hurtful to them, you see – that she would do such an awful thing."

"She was a silly, weak-minded woman!" Reuben Wilcox snarled. "Men die, all the while, and their sweethearts marry other men without a backward look. Why should I have thought she would be any different from a hundred other women?"

"Because she was the hundred and first," Jim retorted, "And believed at once in the easy lie that you told for your own advantage." To his mild surprise, Mrs. Nichols set aside the bowl of shelled peas, swept up the empty pods in her apron, and brought herself up to her full banty-hen height, facing the unfortunate Mr. Wilcox, who topped her by at least a head and a half.

"You may call her silly and weak-minded," she snapped, with an expression in her eyes which would not have been misplaced in that of a man facing another man over a pair of aimed dueling pistols. "Which I misdoubt, but she would have inherited half of a handsome property adjoining your own; that was the attraction, I judge. You thought to take advantage and edge out our Jeremiah by telling vile tales like a sneaky schoolboy? Well and all, Reuben Wilcox, once the story of this gets out, you won't be able to court a girl of a decent family anywhere within miles of Bastrop. Good day to ye. You and your corn are not welcome at this place, once I tell Nichols of this conversation."

"It's a pity that there is nothing in Blackstone which suggests that a charge might be brought against someone maliciously passing on a falsehood which inspires a suicide," Jim mused, some days later as he and Toby jogged down the road which would eventually bring them to Bexar. "There is always slander and libel – which can hardly be brought to bear on this case, though."

"There is nothing in your law which may bring Reuben Wilcox to account," Toby agreed, pacing Jim's horse easily. "But he has come under the judgment of a higher authority and found guilty and wanting – by the older women of the village. For that judgment has no appeal, and no mercy."

2 – The Borderlands Beast
The Second Adventure

Wherein Jim and Toby take to the wilds, hunting a strange creature that is attacking residents of the borderlands around Laredo – a man or a beast?

"It's the damnest thing," Jack Hays mused. "Here I have a letter from our friend Mr. Biddle in Laredo, passing on tales of a strange hairy beast supposedly attacking, mutilating and murdering people – and now I read the same thing in the *Telegraph & Texas Register* and by a completely different correspondent... Is there some kind of moon-madness afflicting people down along the Rio Grande? Or has everyone there begun eating locoweed stewed in aguardiente?"

"No idea," Jim replied, as Jack handed him the folded sheets of the *Telegraph & Texas Register*. They were sitting at a table out back of a saloon and beer-garden on Soledad Street, in the oldest part of Bexar. The establishment – narrow and dark, presented a fortress-like aspect to the street and ran down to the river edge, fringed with rushes and shaded by immense old cypress trees. The proprietors of the saloon/beer-garden had set out rough tables and chairs under the trees. It was just twilight of a mild spring day, and the oil lamps hanging from lower tree branches cast a pleasant golden glow; just enough between their light and sunlight fading from the pale sky to read the tiny print of the newspaper. At the riverbank, lightening-bugs flashed their tiny brief lights among the rushes.

"… fleeting glimpses of an immense, shaggy black shape, nimbly leaping from wall to tree, leaving the victim, one Augustine Santiago sprawled on the ground, dismembered and hideously mutilated about the face, his throat chewed through as if by razor-sharp teeth set in a monstrously strong jaw …" Jim shook his head. "And his right arm torn entirely off his body. It would take inhuman strength to perform that feat. I've heard a lot of stories about what the Comanche get up to when the devil is in them and they have an enemy to torture – but I've never heard anything this outlandish. I suppose one of those enormous grizzly bears could mutilate a man in that fashion with their great claws, but the description of the beast moving and leaping from trees and high walls sounds like anything but a bear – and if there are any bears of that nature around these parts, I've yet to hear of them. What does Albert Biddle have to say?"

"Only that this Santiago murder is the latest," Jack replied, unfolding the pages of the letter from Laredo. "And Biddle is a sensible man, not given to megrims and alarms…"

"Who was this Augustine Santiago?" Jim wondered aloud. He had not gotten that far in the newspaper.

"A Mexican merchant with a large mercantile establishment in Nueva Laredo and a *finca* on the Texas side of the river … distant kin to Dona Graciela, which is why your friend wrote to me. There is more than has been put in the newspaper, you see. Biddle writes that several young shepherds in the vicinity have been found dead, and savagely mutilated in much the same manner. The common folk blame the Indians … but the condition of the bodies is so different from we have been accustomed to see in our various wars with the wild tribes – this is a most curious matter. It seems," Jack cleared his throat, meaningfully, "That this murderous beast has likewise been preying upon them, also. Those in Laredo of Biddle's acquaintance who maintain friendly relations with certain of the Comanche and Lipan and others claim that the Indians are frightened as well – frightened almost out of their skins, telling tales of flying death bats and cannibal skulls with wings, and child-sized monsters with a taste for human flesh. Significantly, they blame the white man, or alternately the Mexicans for bringing the monster into the region. The Mexicans and the Americans, of course, are equally eager to blame some mad renegade among the Indians – as if there was any excuse needed to set all parties at each other's throats. I'd like to put out this little bonfire before it grows any bigger. Since you and Mr. Shaw have the friendship of Old Owl and his Penateka folk, I'm tasking you with going to go to Laredo and discovering what you can regarding this monstrous man-killing beast … and if possible, put an end to it. Show off the pelt in the market-place, so that everyone knows the matter is settled."

"Give us a day or so to pack our traps," Jim replied. "And plenty of lead… do you know – there was a man-killing wolf which supposedly killed and ate a hundred people in Southern France, in the days of one of the Louies? It was eventually shot and killed by a hunter using a special silver bullet which had been blessed by the local priest. Do you suppose I should take that kind of precaution, Jack?"

"If you chose to do so, pay out of your own purse for it," Jack replied. "In my experience, cold lead with black powder behind it has been fitting enough to do the job of putting an end to a murderer, no matter if it goes on four legs or two."

The next day, when Toby Shaw appeared at Jack's quarters in an old adobe house on Main Plaza, Jim's Indian blood-brother listened to Jack outline the new mission with a wholly impassive expression on his face. When Jack had finished, Toby shook his head.

"This sounds like a monster, such as the Old Ones of my people called a 'wendigo'. This is a very dangerous creature to hunt, according to the old tales. I have no relish for this hunt – but as you say – this is a perilous matter. The wendigo is an unnatural thing, leaving no tracks by which a man might hunt it. But it sounds as if this is a living thing – and living things leave prints in the dirt by which they may be followed. Only …" Toby paused, and it unsettled Jim, how Toby's hand had gone to fiddle with the star-iron talisman at his throat, a piece of unearthly metal the size of a pecan-meat, strung on a thong about his blood-brother's neck, as it had been since the very first day of their meeting, at the scene of a bloody ambush in the Nueces strip.

"Only – what?" Jim said, and Toby shook his head.

"Nothing, Brother. Only this matter has the stink of a great evil about it. I will send a message to our Comanche friends, asking Old Owl to meet with us somewhere near Laredo."

Three days later, Jim and Toby set out for Laredo, bearing with them a letter on heavy paper with Jack's signature, authorizing them to make inquiries on both sides of the border. Jack had signed it with an especially impressive flourish, with his official title, and the official seal of the Republic embossed below.

"That should open some doors, in Nueva Laredo, at the very least," Jack said, as he handed it to Jim on the morning of their departure. "Don't know if it will impress the Penateka or the Lipan, much – for that, you and Shaw need to depend on your own swift wits and clever line of palaver. Good luck. And when you kill this beast … bring me a souvenir; a scalp, or a set of claws, or teeth; something that I can put on the shelf and brag about to folk."

Jim sensed his blood-brother's continuing doubtful thoughts about this mission, although forbore to speak of it, until they were well on the trail toward Laredo, and the ramble of Bexar, punctuated by the blunt dome of San Fernando had diminished by distance at their backs. Spring rains falling on the gentle rolling hills and grasslands had brought forth a bounty of wildflowers – blue buffalo clover, purple verbena, pink wild primrose, and yellow tickseed in such numbers that in places, the green grass was overpainted with blossoms. There was no sound other than that of the wind soughing in the grass, and the pleasant regular clopping of their horses' hooves, and that of the single pack-mule following them.

"This is a dangerous hunt, Brother," Toby said at last. "More dangerous than any search we have undertaken before. Whether it is an evil of this world, the world of men who walk in the light of the sun, or from the spirit world … we must be very careful. This wendigo has greater powers than any of which I have ever heard."

"I don't think that the Beast is anything other than of this world," Jim replied, trying to hearten himself as well as his blood-brother. "Of this world in the here and now. Ghostly apparitions do not appear out of the ether, and tear and rend human flesh with anything other than earthly talons and teeth. Depend on it – this is some animal, perhaps a wild catamount, or a wolf with a taste for human flesh. There is no danger to us, being armed and doubly wary."

"It is the most curious thing," Albert Biddle confessed some days later. "I don't think it is anything like a bear, or even a wolf. Perhaps a panther of enormous size and ferocity." It was after supper, on the evening the day that Jim and Toby arrived in Laredo, and were made welcome in the rambling old-fashioned house that Albert shared with his wife, Dona Graciela, her daughters, and her small nephew who by chance had become the godson of Albert, Jim and Toby. Now the boy was a sturdy three-year-old, and had yielded up his infant cradle to Albert and Dona Graciela's new baby daughter – but even the obligations of a new mother had not diminished the serenity of Dona Graciela one bit, or her boundless hospitality toward guests who were the particular friends of her American husband. Proud and as gracious as her own name suggested, she was of the old high-born blood of Spain, not the least diminished by a century of self-exile to the farthest frontier of old Mexico.

"You have not seen the borderlands Beast with your own eyes?" Jim asked, as the cathedral bells of San Augustin chimed the hour for sundown Vespers. They sat in comfortable rawhide chairs in a covered arbor which overlooked a small garden, enclosed within the walls and covered galleries of the house. Water tinkled in the fountain at its center, and nourished the lush growth of ferns and lilies around it.

"No, but I questioned the servants at the Santiago *finca* most closely, when word reached us," Albert replied. "It all sounded most mysterious, and of course, Gracie – my wife – was distraught. Don Augustine was among her favorites, among her first husband's kin. He had traveled widely and was of broader interests than most – and certainly of broader toleration of the modern world. He had many books, curiosities, as well as a menagerie of pets gathered through his travels. Gracie has often said that many of her countrymen – that is, of her kin before consenting to honor me by becoming my wife – were appallingly medieval in outlook. As if they had gotten as far as the sixteenth century and refused to go any farther."

"I think that we should begin our investigations at the Santiago residence," Jim suggested, as Dona Graciela herself came into the arbor where they conferred, after enjoying a bountiful supper. "Can that be arranged, Ma'am Biddle?"

"Of course," Dona Graciela exchanged a brief kiss with her spouse. She had a black lace veil arranged in the Spanish fashion over a tall comb set in her dark hair, and her rosary in her hands. "Alberto, it is time for Vespers. I shall speak to my cousins, and the cousins of my first husband, if any are in attendance tonight. Are you attending prayers with me?"

"No, my heart. I have much to discuss with my friends regarding the matter of the ravaging beast," Albert took her hands in his, and pressed them to his heart. "Ask for a prayer for us, *mi esposa*, in this endeavor. Tell those who ask, that my friends have come to Laredo at the express request of the government of the Republic of Texas to investigate the matter of the ravaging beast."

"I will, *querido esposo*, since the government of Mejico cannot do that much for us in that respect and your friends have proved fortunate in so many previous ventures." Dona Graciela left the garden, trailed by her two daughters and the duenna who attended on them, and the three men returned to their discussion.

"I will arrange it so that you may pay a visit to the Santiago residence in the next few days," Albert Biddle, who had stood at the approach of his wife, now resumed his chair. "And introduce you to those of this town and locality who have seen the Beast with their own eyes. It is a sad thing," Albert added with a sigh. "Nearly half those known to have been killed by it were children or youths – set to herd goats and sheep in the fields, sometimes within sight of their parents. One poor woman was attacked in her own garden, harvesting late pumpkins – this was last fall, of course. As near as I can determine, that was the first of the murders, of which note was taken locally. Don Augustine was slain three or four weeks ago, after telling his friends that he was undertaking his own investigation. There may not be a full accounting of the victims, though. There were a few whose remains were refused proper Christian burial by Father Jose, as there was so little left to find of them, once the beasts and the wild scavengers had done their worst. It may be that some have not been reported, yet buried privately. It was told to me that the body of one poor child – a hunter of the Beast wished it to be left alone, as bait for the Beast. The parents were distraught, naturally, and refused."

"And there is no accounting of how many have been slaughtered among the People of the Apache or the wandering Comanche hunters," Toby mused, a thoughtful expression. "I will await Old Owl's messenger – I have no doubt that he and his kindred are near at hand. He is the wisest and most respected of their Old Ones. Just as he came to be to where we first met and swore the oath of blood brotherhood for our protection."

"I have never heard the story of that," Albert Biddle looked interested. "I have always wondered…"

"It was a matter over which we were sworn to secrecy, a matter of overwhelming national interest," Jim replied, apologetically. Albert, who had been deeply involved in certain matters of that sort on behalf of his own nation nodded in complete understanding.

"Tomorrow, or the following day," Dona Graciela reported, on her return from Vespers. Her daughters had retired to their own chamber, escorted by their duenna, and hers and Albert's baby daughter slept in a basket at their feet, after Albert had dandled her in his arms, and told her what a pretty girl she was, and would be, once that she was grown. Dona Graciela beamed with pride. She settled into her chair, and lit a small cigarillo against the mosquitos which haunted the garden after twilight. The mild smoke from her husband's cigar melded in the early evening, and assured some freedom from the whining and almost invisible flying creatures. "Don Augustine's favorite nephew, Anselmo – he is in residence in the *finca*, and will offer hospitality. All of the old servants have remained. He was such a charming man, Don Augustine. He told us so many interesting tales of his travels – into the Levant and Africa – even as far as China, on several voyages. Cousin Anselmo, he cherishes the memory of Don Augustine, even as I do." Dona Graciela exhaled, a small breath of mild-scented tobacco, and briefly appeared mournful. "He was such an accomplished gentleman – and so devoted to his pets. Cousin Anselmo assures me that they will all be cared for, most devotedly."

By which Jim assumed that the pets were of the nature of cats, perhaps some cherished hunting dogs, or even a gaily-hued parrot – he was correct regarding the parrot, but little else. Don Augustine's *finca* was a sprawling establishment some little way west of Laredo, just out of sight of town, with the squat tower of St. Augustin amid a huddle of looming cottonwood trees dipping their thirsty roots deep into the soil along the riverbank. The *finca* was itself almost a village; a village of small adobe houses and small gardens arranged in an open square with patches of corn already knee-high in small gardens enclosed to keep away the hungry goats and calves. There was even a tiny chapel with a single bell hanging in an arched opening above the door. Children played in the outer courtyard, among wandering chickens and goats.

"This has the look of a prosperous place," Jim observed judiciously, as he rode with Toby and Albert toward the largest house, which took up one side of the square. The massive doors – more suitable to a fortress stood open, and welcoming. Albert nodded.

"It is. Don Augustine held property on both sides of the river, plus the larger portion of his mercantile interests, and a pair of steamships transporting goods and cattle between Matamoros and Cuba … it was always something of a mystery to me why Don Augustine chose to live in retirement here, when had so many other choices. Gracie told me it was because of his menagerie … which includes an enormous tortoise and a tame ocelot. He preferred their company to that of other humans, mostly."

"Good heavens – really?" Jim ventured. "This I must see for myself. I had little expected this part of Texas to contain a peaceable kingdom."

A young man appeared in the open doorway, a very young man in a fine-cut suit of black cloth trimmed with silver buttons in the style favored by Mexicans of good family. He greeted Alfred as if a familiar friend, and turned to Jim and Toby with grave attention when Albert elaborated on the nature of their errand. Jim, studying the bearing and manner of their host, thought that although he seemed very young, barely more than a boy, at first – yet he conducted himself and spoke as if accustomed to responsible authority far beyond those years. A servant relieved them of their horses, and they followed Don Anselmo into the large house, through a large salon sparsely furnished with chairs, and a single long table. Like those houses of the old style in Bexar, the main house was built around an open courtyard, a single row of rooms opening onto a loggia or covered arcades which did the service of a hallway. The only ornament in the room through which they were led was an enormous painted portrait hanging over the simple fireplace.

"My uncle," Don Anselmo gestured toward the portrait – an imposing gentleman of certain years, seated in a tall chair, as if a throne. A red and blue feathered bird with a long tail perched on the back of the chair, and several other animals – a large tortoise, an ocelot kitten played at his feet with a ball, and a tiny, big-eyed monkey sat in his lap, leaning against him for all the world like a small child in the arms of a loving parent. "And some of his animals – he was devoted to his menagerie – from Africa, and the islands, even the far east. My own father used to say that Tio Augustine only paid attention to his business concerns for the sake of collecting more animals."

"Singular," Jim murmured, and Don Anselmo smiled.

"Come, let us sit outside in the shade – it is such a pleasant day – and I will answer your questions regarding the death of my uncle, and those poor others blamed on the Beast"

They followed Don Anselmo through the room, and out through the door opposite, where Jim marveled at the scene. The courtyard and arcades surrounding it housed a selection of Don Augustine's menagerie. An enormous turtle, the size of a bushel-basket or a small boulder crawled deliberately across the sunniest portion of the courtyard, and blinked sleepily at them all, as it chewed on several new and tender leaves of cactus, piled in a shallow basin. A pair of black and white spotted lizards reposed in a small latticed enclosure, in the shade of the arcade. A gorgeously-colored bird – blue and red, with a long tail – of what breed Jim did not know, perched in the lower branches of the lemon tree, squawking now and again in a raucous voice which sounded unnervingly human. And what Jim first assumed was a round seat cushion made of brown-dotted yellow fur on the largest chair, moved, and stretched, regarding them through half-slitted eyes; a live ocelot, as large as a small dog. Like a dog, the ocelot wore a studded collar. It regarded them for a long moment, while Jim held his breath, then yawned – displaying a row of very sharp teeth and a long pink tongue – and resumed its nap.

"It is good to know of this interest taken by such an important man as Captain Hays," Don Anselmo confessed, as he gestured them toward the other comfortable chairs set underneath a loggia which sagged under the weight of heavy grapevine stems, stems newly adorned with new green leaves. "We pray hourly that this beast may be hunted to ground … those who go out with their sheep and goats now fear to go from the sight of their own houses. Please, come sit with me under the arbor. May I offer you some refreshment – you must be thirsty, for the day is already warm."

"That would be most welcome," Jim said gratefully. At a nod from Don Anselmo, an older woman in a dark dress withdrew into the house, returning in moments with a heavy tray; cool lemonade, sweet and tart all at once – obviously made from the fruit of the large tree in the corner of the courtyard, whose blossoms perfumed the morning air. "And tell me if you have seen this creature with your own eyes. Describe it as best you can."

"I have only seen it from great distance," Don Anselmo answered readily. "We followed the tracks from where one of the herd-boys was killed – the child was the third or fourth killed by this monster. My uncle and I rode out as soon as word was brought to us of the killing, with one of our men who is a good hunter, trying to find a trail. It was most difficult, Señor – broken in many places, especially when passing among trees. There were so many tracks, broken and smudged – now and again looking somewhat like the footprint of a barefoot man with a crippled toe and sometimes like the handprints of a man. It was a broken trail, señors – and nearly impossible to follow. But my uncle and I, and our tracker, together we persevered, until close to the end of the day we came to a stand of trees where the river makes a bend to the north, and then south again, like the neck of a bag, with the opening of the bag to the south. And there ..." he paused to gather his thoughts and memories, "We spied a dark figure among the trees ... running like an animal on all fours, at first, and then standing as tall as a man, leaping into the tree branches ... and that was where we lost the trail, although we quartered that grove, searching for any sight of the Beast."

"What do you estimate of the size of the Beast?" Jim asked, reverting to his lawyer-like quest for precision."

"About the size of a man," Don Anselmo replied, readily. "A heavy-set man of perhaps fourteen or fifteen stone, but dark – as black as a Negro, I think. Of amazing strength, besides; it sprang up into the nearest tree as we watched from a distance – and vanished." We could find no further trace of the Beast, although we searched the woods until it became too dark to see."

"Was your uncle attacked and killed by the Beast then?" Jim asked, and Anselmo shook his head.

"No – that happened several weeks later. My uncle had ridden out almost daily, searching the Beast himself, against all advice and warning. He was an old man, señors but feared nothing. By chance, some of the Beast's tracks were made in a wallow, close to the Creek of Saint Ysabel, somewhat west of here, where the mud was soft enough to make them clear. We brought a shallow dish from the kitchen and lifted out the clearest of those prints to show to others, that they might know the marks. I have let them dry completely – let me know you."

Anselmo rose from his chair, leaving the three friends to relish the lemonade, and the prospect before them – the tortoise placidly munching on cactus pads, the bird squawking to itself in the lemon tree, and the ocelot basking in the puddle of sunshine which happened to fall upon the chair in which it lounged.

"What do you think?" Albert Biddle murmured, as soon as Anselmo had gone within. Jim replied, "I honestly do not know what to think. This Beast is so beyond the ken of anything I have ever seen on the frontier … and it has the potential to do so much damage, setting three or more peoples against each other. Never mind the tragedy of those poor children savagely murdered while at their simple chores… I would indeed like to hear what Old Owl says of this, indeed I would."

"I hope to hear from him soon," Toby's countenance was set in its usual inscrutable expression. "His medicine is strong, and he has never failed us before."

In a few moments, Don Anselmo returned, carrying a round pottery dish, saying, "This is the best and clearest of the footprints the Beast left in mud."

Jim and Toby looked into the dish, and the rough disk of hard-dried mud, with the large footprint impressed into the center.

"I think it looks most like a man's bare foot, a man with a deformed large toe." Jim ventured at last, while Toby considered the print with fixed and silent concentration. "I assume that this is the Beast's right foot? Is the left foot deformed in this manner as well?"

"Yes, as near as we could see," Don Anselmo replied.

"Curious, most curious," Jim mused. "Well, I'll know it again, when I see it," and Toby nodded in assent, just as that woman servant who had brought the lemonade appeared in doorway, speaking in soft Spanish to Don Anselmo and Albert Biddle.

"It appears that there is a message come for you," Don Anselmo finally said. "The son of one of my tenants says that it is from 'los Indios' – and asks for the man known as the Far-Walking One and his white blood-brother. The boy will take you to the man who has brought the message to him. He waits in the grove by the river."

"Thank you for your hospitality," Jim rose from his chair. "But we have been waiting for this messenger. The assistance of ... certain friends among the Indians may be invaluable in tracking down this Beast. From our information, this monster may be attacking them as well – and who may know the wilderness better than those who claim to command it entirely?"

"Until we meet again, Señors," Don Anselmo bowed, most courteously. "And if I may be of any assistance to you in this matter, you need only send me word. My uncle is – was – most dear to us, and I must consider the welfare of his people. Put an end to this Beast, I beg of you."

"We will do what we can," Jim returned the bow.

The boy was waiting for them, just outside the main door to the house – a shy small Mexican boy who barely whispered a dozen words to them before Don Anselmo's groom returned with their horses. They set off following the boy on foot – through the scattering of small houses, outbuildings, and cultivated fields, toward the river. There looked to be a stand of trees a little distant, spindly hackberry and live oaks clustered on the brow of a low rise. They did not see the man who waited for them there, until he moved from the shadows at the foot of a tree in the heart of the glade, a man with a blanket around his shoulders that was almost the same shade as the earth; a young man, whose sun-bleached light hair hung in braids below his shoulders, and dressed in the brief manner of a Comanche warrior. Jim, Toby, and Albert had shared a small adventure with this man and his war party the year previous, at the old ruined Spanish fortress in the San Saba country.

"Old Owl waits for you," said Lions the white Comanche, as casually as if they had just met in the streets of Bexar after a short time apart. "I am your guide. Make haste."

"Good to see you again," Jim remarked to Lion's back, as the small boy vanished, pelting away as if he was in the deepest fear of the Comanche – which he might well have been. The Comanche raided as heavily in the farmlands and ranchos along the Rio Grande as they did everywhere else. Lions replied with a nearly soundless snort which could have been either acknowledgment or disgust. His pony was tied to a tree on the far side of the grove – Lions untied it, and sprang effortlessly onto his back, not even looking back at them, as he led them, straight as an arrow north. Jim and the others followed as best they could, not without some apprehension. They might put trust in Old Owl, Mopechucope of the Penateka, and Lions was not an enemy, as these things went … but the toleration of the other Penateka Comanche was a variable commodity.

As on the occasion of their first meeting, Old Owl sat tranquilly before a tiny fire in the shade of a dusty green saltbush shrub; a wiry, wizened old man, whom the harsh life of the wild Comanche had weathered to agelessness. He waited as if he had all the time in the world, while Jim and the others tied up their horses to the nearest red-branched manzanita. Lions gestured them to sit in a half-circle before the old medicine man. Knowing that he would not have sent for them unless the matter was of importance to the Comanche as well as anyone else, they waited without showing any sign of impatience, for that would be a discourtesy to the man who – more than any other in the world – guaranteed the friendship of the Comanche toward Jim Reade and Toby Shaw. Finally, the old man began to speak, waiting at leisurely intervals for Toby to offer a translation.

"There has been much talk regarding the murderous *sarii-*creature among our people. It is a matter of wonder to us, such a thing as we have never seen before in all our wanderings. Not a wolf, not a bear – a warped man-like thing. Black fur like to a bear, but somewhat man-shaped. Immensely strong, able to fly among the branches of trees. A woman of our people gathering wood was killed by this demon-thing in the time of the last full moon. Butchered as we butcher an antelope or a rabbit. Torn apart. It has strength greater than that of any of our people. We have never seen such as this. Is this something that the *tekwapu* have brought among us?"

"No – this was not something brought by our people," Jim relayed through Toby. "For we are as baffled as your wise ones. We have been sent by our great chief to put an end to the Beast, by whatever means are required."

"It is not a thing of this world," Old Owl replied, through Toby. And Jim replied, "But it has made tracks; draw them in the dust, Brother, as Don Anselmo showed us. The Beast is of this world, most assuredly – for a spirit or a demon would leave no trace at all. Living things leave marks where they have been."

He and Old Owl watched, keenly, as Toby, frowning in concentration, dribbled a little water out from the gourd at his side, and then drew and molded in the dampened soil between them, the exact image of the Beast's footprint preserved in the mud, which Don Anselmo had thought to save. But even that sunbaked image in hard clay could not be as exact as Toby's peculiar memory, upon which were imprinted anything which he had looked upon and studied, as an odd kind of mental daguerreotype. Old Owl nodded – as near as Jim could see – with an expression of recognition on his weather-wrinkled countenance.

"Old Owl says that yes, this is the exact footprint of the *sarii* which has haunted the thickets and trees by where the chief of the *kahni*, the great house near this place was slain. His people have often seen this mark in the dirt. It is as if the *sarii* is bold and arrogant, with no wish to hide the marks that it makes. He asks if we are going to hunt it to earth, or wherever it makes a lair, and kill it – so that it no longer haunts this earth."

"We will do so," Jim replied. "It is our sworn oath to kill this Beast. Does the respected Old Owl know where it might be found? Know where it makes a lair to shelter and sleep, where it prefers to drink and hunt? It must be a creature of habit, seeing that it has only killed within a small area."

Jim waited patiently for Toby to relay the question and answer, meanwhile aware that at his elbow, Albert Biddle could not entirely conceal his restless impatience. "If we know the range which the Beast prefers, we may simply search until we cross its' most recent trail. Why must we waste time on palavering with a man who thinks the Beast is a supernatural being?"

"There are more things in heaven and earth, Horatio, than are dreamt of in our philosophy," Jim murmured in reply. "Old Owl may not know of the Bard of Avon, but he does know of those things, and I am inclined to consider his advice. Shussh, Old Owl speaks."

The old man spoke at length, and to Jim's relief, Albert kept a respectful silence. At the end of it, Old Owl brought out from the blanket over his shoulders a small leather bag and gave it to Toby, who accepted it with every evidence of respectful awe. At last, Toby said, "He will work a blessing for us, that we may be guided and protected. He has given me a bag of special dust, to throw at the creature, should we be caught by surprise – as it appears so many have been."

"Ridiculous gesture," Albert commented, but in a low voice. "Does he think that we are ignorant heathens? Just tell us where the Beast ranges, and we will take care of the rest."

"The *sarii*-thing which makes these footprints haunts a lowland west of here – where the great river makes a bend like a large pouch to the north, and a smaller creek empties into it ..."

"The Santa Ysabel Creek," Albert Biddle said at once. "I know that place – it's about half a day's ride from here, along the river. So, the Beast has his haunt there; I might have thought as much, from stories told among Gracie's servants. Should we continue today, gentlemen, or make a fresh start in the morning."

"In the morning," Jim made his decision, although Albert Biddle looked disappointed. "I wish to make certain of sufficient ammunition – and to invite Don Anselmo to accompany us, as well as any reliable, cool-headed men of town who you know to be good at following a trail, and crack shots as well. With just the three of us, there is too much chance of an animal as wily and strong as the Beast to slip away, or even overpower us." Jim considered in silence, while Lions and Old Owl waited with equal patience. He must come up with a plan – a plan to corner the Beast in the sparsely-settled valley of the big river, a Beast which had been hunted by a bare handful of men before. Finally, Jim turned to Albert Biddle and Lions.

"Draw me a map of this place where the Beast hides – start with the grand river, at the confluence of Santa Ysabel Creek. I have a plan for cornering the Beast so that it cannot elude the hunters – if Old Owl's people may assist, beginning at the hour of the day when the sun is the width of a man's hand above the east horizon."

The plan came even more clear to him, as Lions and Albert Biddle scratched in the oval of dirt before them, Old Owl adding his corrections in his reedy voice. Finally, the map was completed, just as the considerations in his own mind arranged themselves into a plan.

"Listen, then," Jim said at last. "This is what we are going to do."

The party from Laredo rode out before dawn, twenty strong and every man in it laden with every weapon he owned, and fresh-cast lead bullets in plenty. Albert Biddle called upon certain of his neighbors whom he knew to be fit and trusty men, Anglo and Mexican, or even of mixed heritage, men of some experience as soldiers. Don Anselmo met the party at the road which branched off the main track to his *finca*, a half-dozen of his vaqueros at his back. They were a rough and ruffianly lot, lightly armed and well-mounted on nimble mustangs of the breed best-accustomed to working the wild and wide-horned cattle of the countryside. Two of them carried long lances, in the manner of *ciboleros*, those who hunted buffalo on horseback armed with nothing more than a spear. Jim thought, with grim humor, that his little army of Beast-hunters made a company of even more motley than a party of Rangers, between the vaqueros and the *ciboleros*, the neatly-suited Yankee townsmen, and the soft-spoken Kentuckian who wore a fringed buckskin hunting coat and a cap made of fur, and carried a rifle across his saddle which was longer than he was tall.

"The bottom lands where the Beast hunts is thick with trees," Jim warned the Kentuckian. "Best take care that you don't hit one of the Indians beating the bush by accident."

"Son," the Kentuckian looked at him levelly and spat into the dust at his horses' feet. "I ain't missed a shot with this-here rifle since I was knee-high to a grasshopper."

"Let's keep it that way," Jim replied. "From what I have heard – we will only have once chance for a shot at it, anyway."

At the confluence of the creek with the river, Jim gathered the party around him for last instructions. The sun was now the width of a man's palm above the eastern horizon, sending long shadows across the rolling prairie and scrubland. "Half of you go with Don Anselmo. Cross the creek and spread out on the far riverbank – but not so far that you cannot see the man to the right or left of you. The last man on the western flank, wave a handkerchief when he is in position. Pass the signal along, so that I will know when you all are in place. We cannot let the Beast escape by slipping through the cordon." He waited for Don Anselmo to repeat this in Spanish to his men. "The Beast has slain Comanche and Mexican alike – and on this day, we three peoples have a common enemy. For this day there is a truce declared. The Comanche will do their part, and we will do ours." He fixed the Laredo men and Don Anselmo's vaqueros with the sternest expression that he could command. "Tomorrow, perhaps, the war between us and the Comanche may begin anew – but for today, we are allies. Turn aside from the temptation to shoot or stab at a Comanche, I beg you all."

In obedience to Jim's word, Don Anselmo, his vaqueros and eight townsmen, including the sharp-shooting Kentuckian wheeled their horses, and splashed through the knee-deep waters of Santa

Ysabel Creek. Just above the confluence of creek and river, Jim took out his pocket watch and studied the slow regular movement of the minute hand. At his elbow, Toby murmured,

"You think this plan will work, my Brother?"

"It does when animals or birds are frightened from their grazing or from their perches by men shaking blankets or beating the bushes with sticks, and driven toward other men with weapons in their hands," Jim replied. "In the marshes in the east hunting waterfowl, in the great Western desert for buffalo, or the highlands of Scotland hunting stag. I see no reason why that method should not work here. I have been thinking about it, you see. The Beast has ravaged all this time because those hunting it did so, with one or two in a party. They did not have a strategy like this."

"If it escapes this time," Toby remarked, "You will have a lot of explaining to do to our friends and the gentlemen of Laredo,"

"If it does," Jim's resolve hardened. "Then we will come back and hunt again, to the same plan." He had taken to heart Don Anselmo's account of the children rent into pieces by the Beast, and by the sight of black-clad women laying flowers on new graves in the burial ground next to the chapel at Don Anselmo's *finca*. "I have the authority vested in me by my commander and the nation of Texas. Put an end to the ravages of the Beast. That is my duty, Brother – and I shall do it, whatever the cost."

"Ah." Toby grinned, slightly sideways. "My Brother – you have never been able to catch the murderer Gallantin; are you certain this is not a hunt of the same nature, in substitution?"

"A hit, a very palpable hit," Jim saw the flash of a snuff-colored handkerchief from the nearest hunter on the far side of the creek. He took out his own, bleached somewhat cleaner by the efforts of the laundress in Bexar who attended to the household laundry in Jack's establishment. In a moment, he spotted the handkerchief-flourish of the next horseman in line.

All in readiness. "No – I cannot hunt to ground the murderer of my brother in blood. But I can do such service as I can. Duty is a hard mistress, as you can attest. Piece by piece, we do justice … bring rightness to things, as you say. Solace to the grieving, justice to the helpless. It is all …".

"A oneness," Toby nodded, in perfect agreement. "So – we are ready to do justice to the Beast?"

"We are," Jim replied. He unshipped his own revolver, fired three measured shots into the air – that was the signal for all to begin.

The sounds of a gun fired carried far into the morning air – far into the north of the great river which divided the two lands. Faintly in the distance, Jim heard the horrific war-cries of the Comanche, a sound intended to frighten anyone, man or beast. Especially this Beast.

"The beaters are coming," he said, with resolute calm. "Thrashing the thickets, sending the Beast into our arms. Be ready now."

From where he and Toby waited, still mounted on their restless horses, the horizon to the north was masked by the sparse woodlands that lined Santa Ysabel Creek. Such trees could only grow where there was sufficient water to support them. Yes, those trees and thickets of lower brush would provide a good refuge for the Beast … how long had it managed to hide in this area? How had it come to be, a creature the like of which no one had ever seen. Jim briefly regretted the death of Don Augustine, who had traveled the world and collected creatures. Perhaps he might have offered some insight, through his knowledge of exotic animals …

"Old Owl's people are moving," Toby said, quietly. His horse shifted, restless. Jim squinted his eyes, to better make out what had drawn Toby's attention … oh, it was a flock of birds, mere dark specks against the blue sky, rising in agitation, then wheeling away, before circling to another stand of trees and settling again. Their cries carried, faint in the distance – no, not birds – that was the eerie yelping of Comanche, wordless and menacing. "See – they are running now. The birds are frightened."

Jim caught a glimpse of color – red the color of a scarlet cardinal, a blanket of the kind the Comanche favored, shaken in vigorous hands at the edge of a stand of trees. His heart beat faster – yes, Old Owl's young warriors were doing their part, as Jim had outlined; moving at a run, making as much noise and agitating the bushes as much as possible, frightening the very daylights out of birds and whatever larger creatures nested and denned along Santa Ysabel Creek. "There!" Jim exclaimed, at a sudden violent tumult in the branches not a hundred yards from where he and Toby waited. "See – there it is – coming this way!"

A shapeless, swift-moving dark shape appeared, seeming to fly from one tree to the next, vanishing into the thicket of brush below, brush violently shaken as the hulking black figure emerged, shambling on all fours, then appearing to rise in the semblance of a man – head, shoulders, impossibly long arms. With a wordless cry, more like the howl of an animal, it ran toward the river. Off to Jim's right, a rifle barked, then another – others of the hunting party had seen it. The Beast howled again, a scream of pure fury. It staggered, hesitated – and loped on, straight toward Jim and Toby. Jim leveled his own long gun – a Springfield musket with a percussion mechanism, more reliable than the flintlock which it replaced – how could he miss, as the Beast leaped down the last slope toward them – a horrific simulacrum of a man, with heavy brows and dark lips baring a mouthful of teeth, teeth more like a dogs' as it roared in agony and menace. The shot deafened Jim and his horse danced sideways, panicked by the Beast more than the gunfire.

"A hit!" Jim shouted, for he had – blood burst from the Beast's enormous chest, but it seemed not to feel pain, and instead launched itself at his horse with another shriek of rage. Jim flung aside the Springfield and drew the first of his Colts, firing at point-blank range until it clicked on an empty chamber, while the Beast raged, clawing at Jim's leg, the top of his boot, and the flank of his horse with inhuman strength. Jim hardly felt pain, in his own rush of fury. Toby shouted as well, leaping from his own saddle; having no liking for fighting from horseback. *Fool Brother!* Jim thought, *What is he doing with that medicine bag! He's liable to be trampled!*

Shouting an incomprehensible war-cry of his own, Toby ducked under the neck of Jim's frantic, shying horse, and flung a handful of reddish dust at the Beast, a handful straight into the horrible gaping mouth, the eyes insensate with fury. The Beast let out another howl – torment and baffled rage all mixed as one – letting go of Jim's leg, just as Toby swung his heavy war-ax. The heavy metal head of the old weapon – the traditional weapon of the war-fighting Lenni-Lenape – landed with a brutal crunching sound of shattering bones. Without a shudder, the Beast crumpled to the ground.

The sudden silence was nearly as deafening to Jim's ears as the howling of the Beast had been. His horse stood with drooping head, shuddering as Jim slid down from the saddle. The leg which the Beast had clawed nearly gave way underneath him, as he clung to his horse, both shivering with reaction.

"We've done it," he heard himself say, in mild surprise more than triumph. "We've killed the Beast." It looked much smaller, now, crumpled lax and loose in the trampled, blood-speckled grass and dust. Not entirely human, not quite animal, or at least, not any animal that he had ever seen. "Damned if I know what it is, though. It might be some kind of monkey, but it's bigger than any that I have ever seen, or ever want to see again." The sight of the teeth gave him goosebumps on his own flesh – those were the teeth that savaged so many poor souls, ripping the life from them. And his leg ached abominably, from where the Beast had clawed at his shin.

"I cannot say either, my Brother," Toby was breathing hard as well. He laid down the war-ax with care, and reached for his own belt-knife. Jim watched, as Toby reached for the little tobacco pouch at his belt. Murmuring words in his own language, Toby threw a tiny pinch of tobacco in each of the four directions, then scattered another over the Beast's body, and tossed the last pinch skywards. Still short of breath, Jim leaned over the huddled body of the slain Beast, his attention distracted by … *What was that, bound tightly around that thick neck, near-hidden by coarse black fur? A collar?* Swiftly, Jim unbuckled it – yes, it had been worn long by the Beast, long enough for the metal-studded leather to have worn galls on that neck.

"It was a pet!" Jim breathed. "Someone brought it here…"

In that instant, he comprehended fully; from where the creature had likely come, and by whom it been brought. It was all in the portrait which hung in the main chamber of Don Augustine's big house. "…when it was very small," Jim added. "And then, when it grew and became uncontrollable, he let it go. And he died through his miscalculation of the temper of his pet." He saw the same understanding in Toby's eyes, that quick nod of complete agreement, as he thrust the collar into the front of his hunting coat. The others of the hunting party splashed through Santa Ysabel Creek, or came from farther along the river, gathering in a curious and triumphant little group, chorusing their own questions. In another moment, Lions the white Comanche walked among them, emerging with four of his fellows from the woods to share in the triumph.

The Beast of the Borderlands was dead – no need for assigning further blame, especially since the man responsible was one of the Beasts' victims. But as they rode back toward Laredo, he hung back to ride next to Toby, and to ask for an answer to a question which perplexed him.

"What was in that medicine-pouch that Old Owl gave you – to throw at the Beast. It certainly had more punch than my first shot at the thing."

"A little wood ash," Toby grinned. "And a great many of those little red peppers … you know, those that are the size of a small bird-eye, yet are so very hot? All ground very fine to a powder. They grow well, around the villages, and the birds eat them and spread them in their droppings."

Jim winced. "I ate a whole one once, when I was a young and foolish child. No wonder the Beast howled!"

3 – Murder Being Once Done
The Third Adventure

Wherein Jim and Toby return to Galveston to assist Jim's lawyer father in determining if one of his clients has committed a murder!

"Something eating at you, hoss – since you got that letter from Galveston?" Jack asked, on a bitter-cold winter evening. Out in the Plaza at the heart of old Bexar, the ice-chilled north winds had swept those tables set up by the most enterprising of the red-pepper stew vendors clear of hungry diners, and all but the most desperate of them had gone home. Every citizen of that town who had a hearth to call their own – no matter how plain, tiny or humble, had retreated to the warmth of a good fire of sweet-smelling mesquite logs. Between missions, as assigned by their captain, Jim and Toby roomed in the small adobe house at the edge of the Plaza, near the squat stone tower of San Fernando – the tallest building in town – and stabled their horses in the ramshackle building behind it. Jack, sometime commander of Texas Rangers was not an exception to the general rule on this winter evening. Jim Reade and his blood-brother, Toby Shaw of the Delaware people, shared his dislike of the cold on this evening; between them, they had spent all too many cold nights, shivering and shelter-less on various journeys and campaigns.

"Only puzzlement," Jim replied, closing the volume of *Blackstone's Commentaries* which lay open on his knee. The fire burning on the tiny plastered hearth and the tin candle-sconce between them barely put out sufficient light for him to make sense of the tiny print. "The letter is from my father ... he has been asked by an acquaintance in Galveston for advice on a deeply personal matter, and he in turn has asked my advice – having none other to confide in, other than my dear mother. She is interested as the matter concerns the death of a woman, a woman that she knew – but not well, since the woman in question was much younger and resident in Galveston only for a year or so. It is not a matter of interest for the Rangers, or the State," he added hastily, seeing Jack begin to frown. "A matter of law and conscience ... and doubts."

"There are always doubts, my Brother, when it concerns a matter of concern to women," Toby added, from where he sat on the shabby hearth-rug, cross-legged in Indian fashion, leaning against the side of the box which held more wood for the hearth. "And what does this woman herself say of the matter?"

"Nothing much, since she is dead and laid in her grave this last half-year," Jim replied. "The matter – as my father outlined it to me – is that her widower wishes to marry again, having settled upon a likely candidate for matrimony. The young lady so honored is not yet completely invested in the prospect of matrimony – at least, not with the man who has asked for her hand. Libby Caperton, and she is just fifteen. Her guardians are even less eager to see their ward hand-fasted to him ... hence their consultation with my father."

"So, what is the problem, precisely?" Jack puffed on his pipe in a desultory manner, and laying it aside, looked into the fire; small orange and gold flames, dancing along the logs, bright spurts appearing as brilliant sparks.

"Certain remarks made to Miss Caperton by the man who courts her have cast considerable doubt on his fitness as a husband in their minds," Jim replied, and frowned. He had spent some hours considering his father's letter, teasing out from those brief words some sense of the puzzling reality hinted at, and from what he recalled of reports of a certain trial published in the *Telegraph & Texas Register* some months previous. It was not any surprise that Jack would have noticed his abstracted state of mind; Jack was like that. Not much got past him.

Now Jack drawled, "For the love of the almighty, Jim, don't tell me that Johnathon Knightley is going courting again, after being acquitted from a charge of murdering his wife on the grounds of self-defense?"

"The very same," Jim sighed. No curious event occurring the length and breadth of the Republic escaped Jack's attention for very long. On those shreds of information made, Jack had divined the very essence of the matter. "It was a terrific to-do among the folk in Galveston," he added for Toby's benefit, as the latter looked extremely puzzled. "There was this man and his wife, who kept a tavern and let rooms to travelers – they were new-come to town, from ... where was it?"

"St. Louis, I have heard," Jack interjected. "The wife was somewhat older than her husband, who is a gallant young buck ... and disinclined to give his full attention to their business, which supposedly made his wife angry with him. They quarreled frequently, in any case. You were off on a visit to your people at Fort Belknap at about the time of this happening, Toby."

Jim nodded. "My mother, otherwise inclined to believe the best of any man or woman, took against Jon Knightley upon hearing someone saying to him that his wife had horse-sense, intending it as a compliment, and Mr. Knightley guffawed and answered to the effect that yes, she did, and the face to match it. My mother despises that manner of unchivalrous behavior. Although," Jim added, "Mother did not wholly approve of Matilda Knightley throwing crockery, iron pot-lids, and a wood-hatchet at her husband when her temper was up. My mother is a firm believer in the policy of a soft answer turning away wrath."

"It made Jon Knightley's tale of self-defense believable to the jury, though," Jack agreed.

Toby shook his head in disapproval. "In that regard, the way among our people is more sensible. Our mothers and wives hold the property. If a man wishes not to continue in marriage, then he is free to leave, and our wives have no need to keep an unwilling husband tied close, to provide for them and for their children."

"In this case," Jim returned to the story. "The jury ruled that Jon Knightley acted in self-defense. There were no actual eyewitnesses to death of Matilda Knightley, although there were plenty who testified that they heard the sounds of a violent quarrel between the two of them in the kitchen behind the taproom one morning, and then the sound of three gunshots ... a single shot, and then two more, some seconds later. Jon Knightley came bursting into the taproom, shouting, 'She shot at me – oh, god, she meant to kill me for sure!' So said all those present in the taproom on being called to testify. Of course, it made a tremendous ruckus. Several of their neighbors and the Knightley's slave man-of-all-work ran into the kitchen at once, finding Matilda lying on the floor between the kitchen stove and the worktable, in a pool of blood with two bullets in her breast. She was already dead ... and in her hand, one of her husband's Paterson revolvers, with one shot fired. He had the other, of course – which had been fired twice."

"What, had they arranged to fight a duel?" Toby asked, much puzzled, and Jim replied,

"According to Jon Knightley, he was in his shirt-sleeves, melting lead over the kitchen fire which had been new-built-up for the day, and casting more bullets when the quarrel broke out between them. She caught up the one which he had just loaded and shot at him at close range. Luckily for him, the bullet pierced his shirt ... and then buried itself in the wall at his back. In a blind rage, he took up the other pistol and fired at her. On the strength of the hole in his shirt, the jury accepted his plea of self-defense, and he was acquitted of murder."

"All this is old news, hoss," Jack refilled his pipe and lit it from a twig held for a few seconds into the fire on the hearth. "So, now the accused-yet-acquitted self-made widower wishes to try his luck at matrimony before a year of mourning is out? Not in the best of taste, but there is no law against it. Why is your father wound up so tight over this now?"

"Because he was Knightley's lawyer," Jim replied. "It was his first serious case when he reopened his law practice after getting out of Perote. He believed honestly in his client's innocence, did his best for him, won an acquittal ... and now he is deep in doubt. My father is a moral man, Jack; now he wonders if he has been taken advantage of by a veritable Bluebeard. As an aside, my mother has no doubts on this score; she is certain that Jon Knightley contrived somehow to murder his wife and escape any penalty for it. Miss Caperton's guardians are Mr. and Mrs. Bell. Friends of our family, particularly my mother; well-trusted, and sincerely worried regarding the welfare of his ward, since she has relayed certain comments which Jon Knightley has made to her."

"Which were?" Jack raised a questioning eyebrow. Jim collected his doubts and concerns all together, answering with care and precision. "Knightley showed her the shirt which was the chief evidence in his defense. He has preserved it as some kind of trophy; we are given to understand, and made boastful mention of how it was used in some unspecified manner to rid himself of his previous wife. He spoke in jest, and Miss Caperton thought nothing of it … at the first. Then he made mention of other wives … something about the conversation made her uneasy … distressed, even."

"Oh, my Brother," Toby spoke from where he sat beside the fire. "There is something of sense in what these women say; the girl and your mother and her friend. Just as the wild hare and the wolves sense danger … so may we, although our natural senses are dulled by safety and what you call civilization. Be alert."

"Always," Jim replied, already somewhat reassured.

"Are we on a hunt, then, my Brother?" Toby asked, in all earnest intent. "I would not be against such a journey, as long as it does not begin tonight."

"You are due some leave from your duties with the Rangers," Jack commented, with a wry twist to his lips. "Spend some little time with your family, Jim. And see if you may unravel this accursed tangle. There'll be no pay and expenses in it – only your peace of mind."

"Thanks, Jack," Jim replied, his heart within him suddenly feather-light, although the thought of that long journey in the winter months between Bexar and Galveston nearly made it sink again.

* * *

The warmth of the welcome more than made up for it, once arrived at the tall white house, sheltered in it's garden of gnarled oaks, with the ramble of outbuildings at the back – the concrete-lined brick water cistern, the stable, the summer-kitchen and the servant's quarters. A chill wind, made chillier by closeness to the gulf waters, rattled the glass windowpanes and made the oil-lamp lights flicker uneasily in the polished lamp chimneys.

"Jemmy, my darling boy!" Jim's mother flung her arms about him, in a most exuberant manner, when she opened to front door to find Jim and Toby on the doorstep, soaked to the skin from the ferry-boat journey from the mainland. The sun had just gone down, and a dismal drizzle was falling

"Mama, no one has called me Jemmy since I was out of small-clothes," Jim protested.

"Come in, come in and get warm by the fire – you'll both of you catch your death, standing outside in the rain and wind!" Emily Reade insisted, and the two meekly submitted to being led inside, into the cozy, firelit warmth of the Reade's tall white house, where the rain beat against the parlor windows in vain. 'Tisking' under her breath, she hung up their dripping outer garments on the hall stand. "Elisha, my dear – look who is home?"

Elisha Reade, poring over an illustrated magazine from the East, looked up and over his wire-framed glasses. "Jim, my boy! You were not expected! And Mr. Shaw as well – welcome, welcome, come get warm by the fire! This is such an extraordinary surprise! Nella will be serving supper at half-past the hour, but in the meantime, you can tell me what brings you home so unexpectedly!"

"We're waiting on Mr. Nichols," Mrs. Reade added. "He has been clerking for your father since mid-summer! I did mention that, didn't I? Such a pleasant young man. Rebecca and the children relish his company very much..." She fluttered away to see to last-minute preparations for supper.

"The Knightley matter, that you wrote about in your last letter," Jim and Toby both found seats close to the fire, gratefully holding out their winter-chilled hands. Winter seemed so much colder by the ocean, than in Bexar, which was merely cold without being so infernally damp. "I'm glad that Jeremiah is considering the law, Pa."

"He is," Mr. Reade answered with an air of satisfaction. "And he has been taking a particular interest in this matter. I expect that he feels such interest because of the sad discovery of the fate of his dear Miss Clarke. He is quite the paragon of chivalry when it comes to the fair sex. Of all the wrongs done in this wicked world, Mr. Nichols sees those done to innocent womanhood to be the worst and most unforgivable."

"He would," Jim answered, hearing the front door open and shut again. The voices of his mother and Fat Nella floated distantly from the kitchen, and the sounds of children's footsteps on the stairs, followed by the more deliberate ones; his sister-in-law Rebecca, and Daniel Reade's children; Young Elisha, his brother Samuel, and their sister Eliza. Jim held them in affection, at least as much for themselves, as for being the wife and children of Daniel Reade, dead by treachery in the Nueces country these three – no, it must be four years now.

The children burst into the parlor, followed by their mother, who exclaimed, "Brother James, Mr. Shaw! How marvelous a surprise! We did not expect you; welcome home – are you to stay for long?"

Jim did notice that Rebecca had put off widow-black, in favor of a dress of a pretty shade of violet. She was an even-tempered and gravely pretty woman of near thirty – his brother Daniel's wife. He kissed her cheek, embraced the rambunctious boys, and took their shy little sister onto his lap, when he sat down again. "I'm given leave to help Father, over the Knightley matter."

"It is a puzzle, indeed," Rebecca agreed. She took a chair nearest the bright-burning oil-lamp on the center table. Her mending-basket sat next to it; she took out a … Jim was not entirely certain what it was, only that Rebecca commenced to mending it with tiny, precise stitches under the brightest light in the room. "I hope that you can find the answer to the puzzle, Brother James. Poor Mrs. Knightley was of an impatient temper, but I just cannot credit that she would – even in a fit of fury – shoot at her husband. That she would do so does not set right with me."

"Be fair, Becky," Elisha Reade replied, as his grandsons settled onto the footstool by his chair. "You disliked the man because he was impertinent to you."

"He was," Rebecca stabbed the needle into her work with more than necessary force, and lifted her eyes from her work, to meet the eyes of both Reade men. "Because he was your client, he … assumed a familiarity with me, on account of my state as the widow of your son. And he also assumed that I was eager to be courted in marriage. Which I may be, at some future time," she added, stabbing her needle into her mending as if she were picturing stabbing something sharper and larger into Jon Knightley. "But most definitely not by a man who makes my skin crawl."

"I did not know of this," Elisha Reade remarked, somewhat startled. "You never complained of his behavior to me."

"There was little need, Father Reade," Rebecca answered, suddenly tranquil. "I am a woman grown, and well able to protect myself from the attentions of a crude and vulgar buffoon like Jon Knightley – was there ever a man more ill-named, do you think?"

"No, I would think not," Jim chuckled, as the outside door opened and shut. In a moment, Jeremiah Nichols appeared in the parlor, his face ruddy and his hair damp from the cold and rain outside, a face brightening with welcome to see the family gathered in the parlor.

"Jim! And Mr. Shaw! This is as welcome a sight as it is unexpected ... Sir, and Mrs. Reade! What an evening – it is even more foul outside this evening than I can ever have thought possible..."

"My son and Mr. Shaw have come from Bexar in response to my letter about the Knightley matter," Elisha Reade explained in low tones, as Rebecca chided her sons.

"Boys, behave!" as Young Elisha and Samuel flung themselves on Jeremiah in happy greeting, like puppies vying for the playful attention of a larger dog. At Jim's side, Toby murmured, "James, I think that the wife of your older brother has already accepted a suitor agreeable to her, although perhaps he is..."

"Circumspect in his attentions?" Jim answered, also in a low voice. "I don't blame him. Rebecca was a good and loyal wife to my brother; she deserves better than a lifetime of wearing black. A chance at love for a living husband, and a good step-father for the boys? I have no objection in the least. Jeremiah is a stout fellow and a good man. Perhaps second chances are a good thing."

"So it is among my people," Toby agreed, with a swift grin, as Elisha Reade asked, in a loud enough voice to be heard over conversation in the parlor, "You are late, Jeremiah – what kept you?"

"By coincidence, a man who came to the office, as I was about to put out the lamp and bar the door for the night," Jeremiah drew up one of the light parlor chairs, close enough that he could speak with Elisha Reade without raising his voice. "About Knightley," he added, with a sideways glance at Toby and Jim. "Glad I am that you two fellows are here. This quiet inquiry of yours, Mr. Reade, is in a powerful danger of going sideways. The man who came to the office just now says that he is the late Mrs. Knightley's younger brother from St. Louis; Septimius Maxwell. He is engaged in the Santa Fe trade, was never close to his sister or her husband. They were orphaned early, and he was taken in by an uncle in the Santa Fe trade, while his sister married after a time. As one may tell from the name, he was the youngest child of his parents, his sister the eldest. There were the only two surviving of their parents' children and so were equal heirs of the estate, which was not substantial – yet not small, either. He is convinced that she was murdered by her husband, after marrying her for her portion of it."

"Oh, my," the senior Mr. Reade murmured. "That has been my growing fear, over the last few months, Jeremiah – even though I cannot deduce how this foul deed was accomplished."

"Neither can young Maxwell," Jeremiah replied, moving the chair closer to the Reade men, and to Toby, so that he could speak in even lower tones. "But he is convinced of it. It seems that Mr. Knightley was a widower when he arrived in St. Louis three years ago. Mr. Maxwell is in possession of some intelligence concerning Mr. Knightley's previous residence in Natchez, and the sad and untimely demise of a wife there."

"And he did not share this information with you?" Jim prodded, and Jeremiah shook his head. "He wishes to meet with us on the morrow. Sir, I think he is of a rash and impatient temper. I extracted a promise from him not to speak of this to anyone else, and most of all, not to frequent the Knightley place of business tonight, on the promise of meeting with us first thing in the morning. He is a very young man, although already well-seasoned by his experiences on the Santa Fe trade."

"We shall indeed do just that," Elisha Reade folded up his spectacles, as Emily Reade appeared in the parlor doorway. "All of us – my son and Mr. Shaw as well. Four heads may be better than one or two, when untangling this unfortunate matter."

"Nella is putting supper on the table," Emily Reade announced, and for the moment, all in the room put their minds to the more immediate and delicious matter of a ham seasoned with cloves and served with brandied peaches, roasted sweet potatoes, and greens cooked with slivers of fat carved from the ham.

The sun rose the following morning attended by a few scattered and briefly pink-flushed clouds. The sky was a clear, rain-washed blue, and a brisk wind capped every blue wave in the Gulf with lacy white froth. Jim had quite forgotten the smell of the salt-sea, and the mewling cries of gulls, hovering on near-motionless wings; now he was reminded of them again. He had spent his later childhood here, when the Reade family came to Texas, upon hearing of opportunities there, in the crowded years before the war for independence from Mexico. He and his father, with Toby and Jeremiah walked together, pulling their warm coats close around them, talking easily of the latest news from the *Telegraph and Texas*

Register, of rumors of this or that in Galveston and Bexar and farther afield.

When they came to the simple frame building on the Strand which housed the offices of E. Reade, Esq. – Atty at Law, there was already someone waiting for them, leaning against the convenient iron post hung with four rings for tying up horses while their owners did business. A capable-appearing young man, Jim noted; lean and sunburnt nearly as dark as Toby. He would have made a good Ranger; months on the Santa Fe trail would definitely fitted him to be an able frontiersman. The young man nodded to Jeremiah, and stuck out his hand to Elisha Reade.

"I presume, sir – that you are Lawyer Reade? Good to meet you, sir. Sep Maxwell."

"Mr. Maxwell," Elisha Reade shook his hand, and took out the office key to open the front door. "My pleasure. Mr. Nichols said that you had information regarding a previous marriage of Jon Knightley ... information that I was ignorant of, previous ... no, let us go in, and you may share it with all of us in strictest confidence. This is my son, Captain Reade of the Texas Rangers, and his guide, Mr. Shaw. They are entrusted with certain matters by the State, matters of the highest confidence. You may speak freely in front of them."

"Thank you, sir," Sep Maxwell fixed them all with his gaze – bitter black eyes under straight brows – and then followed them into the office. Jeremiah unobtrusively cleared several stacks of red-tape-tied folders from the spare chairs inside, and they all settled in the space before the senior Mr. Reade's desk. Jim broke the awkward silence which descended on them all, once this was accomplished.

"You communicated to Mr. Nichols," he ventured, "That Mr. Knightley, husband of your sister Martha, was previously married in another city and that you had reason for suspecting that his wife there had also come to an unfortunate end. Would this be direct knowledge, or merely hearsay?"

Sep Maxwell looked between the other three men, somewhat baffled. Jim cleared his throat. "Would you have directly observed Mr. Knightley and his unfortunate domestic situation in Natchez or is that something which you merely heard about from someone else."

"Someone else, sir," Sep Maxwell replied. "But the fellow that told me was a trusty sort, not given to yarn-telling. His people kept a livery stable in the same street as Knightley, back in Natchez."

"Go on," Elisha Reade made notes in his careful hand. "That person's name, and his present profession?"

"Jobe Zumwalt; a wagon-master with my uncle's freighting concern, Maxwell and Franks. A trustier and more fair-spoken man can hardly be found in the Santa Fe trade. It came about that we were talking around the campfire of an evening about bad-tempered women, and I happened to mention about my sister. Not speaking ill of the dead, o'course – just swapping yarns. I made mention of how my sister got herself killed after shooting at her husband; talking 'bout the importance of peace in the home, you know. I made mention of her married name, and Jobe speaks up, with a curious look on his face. 'Jon Knightley, from Natchez? A big, round-face man, sported chin-whiskers and no mustache, got a round mole on his forehead, just over his left eye?' Well, that sounds like my sister's man, and I say so. Jobe, he looks at the fire and thinks a little, 'afore he speaks up. 'I think I knew that man in

Natchez, seven or eight year gone it was, when I was still living with my folks. I recollect him plain, because of his wife dying.' 'Can't be,' says I. 'My sister and Jon Knightley lived in Galveston these last few years – not Natchez.' And Jobe, he shakes his head. 'No, the Jon Knightley I remember lived with a wife in Natchez, just down the road a piece from my folks. She was a little timid thing, wouldn't say boo to a goose. I heard from my Ma that Mrs. Knightley in Natchez was the daughter of a rich planter up Knoxville way, she ran away to marry him. No accounting for taste, I guess.' 'So what happened to her?' I said…'"

"Nothing good, I would venture," Jim whispered to Jeremiah Clarke, who nodded absently. Toby listened with rapt attention.

"She drowned, so Jobe said. In the creek, two feet of water – fetching water for washing, is what everyone thought at first. But the nearest neighbors, they said that the Knightleys had a nigra servant gal, and what need would she have for fetching water? Knightley, he swore to the coroner that his wife went down to make water-colors of the pretty flowers, which Jobe's ma said didn't make a lick of sense, because she was frightened of snakes, bugs, critters and all. It was a nine-days wonder. There wasn't a mark on Mrs. Knightley – but she was still drownded as dead as a salt mackerel. The coroner finally said it was a case of misadventure, since no one could prove anything otherwise."

"There are men who are misfortunate in their marrying," Elisha Reade observed, skeptically, and Jim replied, "Two wives in a row, through accident and misadventure. It stretches credulity…"

Seb Maxwell looked between them, seeming affronted by this mild touch of levity. "There was another wife, before Knightley came to Natchez, or so Jobe heard from gossip at the time. In Knoxville – that one died sudden-like, too. A rich widow-woman."

"We appear to have a veritable Bluebeard among us, if true." Jeremiah Clarke observed, unknowingly echoing Elisha Reade's words; the first to speak, after a short and horrified pause. "Three wives, all of whom brought him money … and all of them dead after a short period of marriage."

"Rumor and hearsay," Elisha Reade cautioned him. "And it is not in our scope to investigate the deaths of the previous two Mrs. Knightleys – only the most recent sad case of your sister. About which there has been enough quiet talk to raise suspicion, even though he was tried and found innocent on the grounds of self-defense."

Seb Maxwell scowled. "You were his lawyer at that trial, or so I've been told. If he really did murder my sister, after doing away with three other women, what do you propose to do about it? And why should I believe your word, anyway?"

"Because, Mr. Maxwell, we follow the laws when it comes to dealing out justice," Jim kept his voice level with an effort. "Otherwise, there is only personal – and if it comes to the worst – mob vengeance. And that is a mighty club, wielded by a blind man, a club more apt to punish the luckless than to administer true justice."

"If you are thinking of some private vengeance," Elisha Reade looked over his glasses and spoke in mild, and conciliatory tones. "I would urge you to put it out of your mind, young man. We will not be moved by blind passions into exacting vengeance. But the law takes time and patience to work it's ways. The mills of justice grind out exceedingly small, but they do so slowly and in their own time. Have patience, I beg of you."

"Work it how you will," Seb Maxwell gathered up his own hat. "You work your own justice and I will do mine." The door to the office crashed shut behind him, and the four remaining were left to look at each other.

"I hope that he will not do anything rash," Elisha Reade polished his spectacles on an immaculate white handkerchief, while his son and Jeremiah Clarke exchanged a sympathetic glance. Toby Shaw remained impassive and silent.

"He's a young idiot, and a hot-blood, Pa," Jim remarked. "Of course, he will take it personal. Who wouldn't when it's a sister? We'd best move faster on this than your usual legal mills... do you know anyone in Knoxville or Natchez that we can write to, asking for confirmation of what Maxwell's trail-companion told him?"

"I'll see what I can do," Elisha Reade replaced his glasses on his nose and pursed his lips thoughtfully. "I'll write to the keeper of public records to confirm that Jon Knightley had been married, in Knoxville and Natchez. The marriages would have been recorded, also the findings of the cause of death of those poor women. They are reputed to have been women of some means upon contracting marriage with him, so there should be probate records as well. That is a most distressing thought. My dear Emily's friends are revealed to have been most sensible, with their worries concerning Miss Caperton and his attentions toward her."

"He was looking at reeling in another rich matrimonial catch," Jim concluded. He had never met Jon Knightley in person – only seen him casually during his infrequent visits to Galveston – but he had already conceived a strong dislike of the man, based on

Rebecca's opinion of him, and now on this new intelligence. "I wonder what it is about that shirt – the one with the bullet-hole in it. The one that he kept, and showed to the girl ..."

"He is counting coup," Toby Shaw spoke, almost for the first time.

"What?" Both Elisha Reade and Jeremiah Clarke spoke almost at the same time, startled and curious.

"Counting coup – taking credit for a feat of bravery against an armed enemy. It is a thing that the wild tribes do. You know, James – the horse warriors and buffalo hunters who live beyond the frontier. Our folk once also practiced this, which is why I know about it; to strike a harmless blow against an armed warrior – that is the ultimate test of courage. One who does so many times in battle has much honor among his people."

"I don't understand," Jeremiah ventured, his pleasant countenance deeply puzzled, just as Jim nodded. It made sense in an odd and unsettling manner.

"Jon Knightley keeps relics; souvenirs of his marital conquests," he explained. "If the tale of him showing the shirt to Miss Caperton and boasting of how he used it to rid himself of his previous wife is any indication. I reckon that he has other remembrances. He strikes me as the kind of braggart who would. Pa, do we have any notion of where he keeps this shirt? I suppose somewhere in his private quarters in the inn. Is there any means by which we can examine it, minutely?"

"I don't know," Elisha Reade wiped his pen carefully, and corked the inkbottle. He set aside his notebook. "This very day, I will send letters to Knoxville and Natchez, but as I said to our young friend – it is the possible murder of his sister which is our prime concern. What are you considering, Jemmy?"

"A matter of simple observation, Pa." Jim replied. "I have seen – much as I wish that I had not – the bodies of many dead men, and where they lay after being slain, the condition of their clothing, the disposition of their possessions. They died through the application of many instruments; knives, arrows, bullets … I should say no more, Pa. I just have a theory – one that I wish to consider and validate through experimentation. But I would like to see that famous shirt of Jon Knightleys'."

"Say no more, Brother," Toby Shaw rose from his chair. "I will see that you examine that coup-trophy, and any others that come to hand…"

"You are not going to…" Elisha Reade began, honestly flustered, and Jim answered,

"He has his methods, Pa – best not to examine very closely, I think. Leave it to us and hope that we can come to some conclusion before young Maxwell acts intemperately." He and Toby exchanged a look of agreement and a nod which sealed the matter.

"Where are you going?" Elisha Reade asked in something of alarm and Jim and Toby rose from their chairs.

"Shooting practice, Pa," Jim returned over his shoulder, as they went out into the street. "Jack says that constant practice is the key for being a better shot. And I have in mind to conduct a particular experiment." Out in the Strand, Jim and his blood-brother walked together, close so that none could overhear their conversation. "Can you get it … and return without anyone being any the wiser?" Jim asked. "Lest of all, Jon Knightley? All that I need is ten or fifteen minutes without interruption. I had a thought which came to me, but I need to do some testing, first…"

"I will see what can be done, my brother," Toby replied, inscrutable as always. "But likely – not until the end of the day."

"When the taproom is full," Jim nodded. "And until then – a bit of the practice which Jack urged on me will not be time wasted. I will ask my mother for one of Pa's shirts from her rag-bag. Let us walk out to the sand dunes and conduct our experiment, then."

***

"So," Toby observed, an hour and a half later. "What have you seen, from this?"

The two of them stood, a few steps from a crude scarecrow cross-frame of poles, from which hung an extremely ragged linen shirt, formerly belonging to Elisha Reade – a shirt from which some small patches had been cut to mend items of a newer vintage. But there was enough of it remaining to serve, hanging from the cross-pole thrust through the sleeves, as a target for Jim's trusty Paterson revolvers. Although he had not stood off at a distance to remedy his poor marksmanship by the constant practice which Jack had urged upon him. A good few shots had been at close range. As close as the range in which Jon Knightley had exchanged – or claimed to have exchanged – revolver-fire with his wife.

"A curiosity which I had already suspected," Jim replied. He was tired. His shoulders slumped, and his ears rang from the frequent report of his revolvers. "Jon Knightley murdered his wife – his latest wife – that is. But absolute confirmation awaits on my examination of the shirt which he wore, and claimed to prove that was the case."

"And the curiosity you see, James?" Toby squinted at him, against the glare from the afternoon sun, cast on the white sands, where the gentle waves slapped at those same sands, and withdrew with a gentle hiss.

"I will show you the comparison when you have procured Mr. Knightley's shirt," Jim took down the holed shirt from the skeleton poles, and folded it carefully. "I am certain that you, my father and Jeremiah will instantly grasp the implications." And he would say no more on that subject, even as Toby nodded.

"When the taproom is full, I will obtain the shirt for you," he promised. "Along with any other things. James, I fear that this man Knightley is possessed by a bad spirit. I do not doubt that he has killed his wife, or that he has killed other women, for the riches that he brought them. I know this; just as I knew about the wagon, and the tainted gold. But your white-man law does not take such convictions into consideration."

"Nor should we," Jim replied. "Our law requires the evidence of observable phenomena and provable facts, not the spectral testimony of invisible spirits or honestly-felt convictions. If it cannot manifest in a courtroom and swear under oath, it is a matter for religion, rather than law. Otherwise, we would be back in the days of the old Puritans, crediting delusions of spirits and imps, on the say-so of a group of malicious children." He smiled, to take the sting from the implied rebuke, for this was an old argument between them. Truth to tell, he had often been guided by his blood-brother's native instincts when investigating a matter for Jack and the nation of Texas – but never in a court of law, under oath. "Just don't get caught, or leave me having to tell a bold-face lie to cover you,

Brother. Which I would; just that I would prefer that such a question never arise to begin with."

"I never do, James," And Toby grinned. "As long as you do not need to ask searching questions in your law courts. My solemn oath upon it."

"And mine," Jim returned.

As they went from the stretch of sand dune and salt-scrub where they had conducted their experiment, Toby added, "I will likely not dine with you tonight. The busy hours at Knightley's place will afford me the best opportunity to seek out the item that you require,"

"I will make your excuses," Jim replied. "And make such credible. Be careful, Brother."

***

His parents expressed only mild regret at the lack of Mr. Shaw's agreeable company for dinner, although Daniel's boys were markedly disappointed. Jeremiah Clarke, his expression carefully inscrutable, made no comment at all. When Toby appeared in the dining room door, and nodded silently toward Jim, only then did Jeremiah and Elisha excuse themselves from the table. Emily and Rebecca made no protest either; Jim wondered if the women had made some prior agreement.

"I'll tell Nella to set aside a slice of buttermilk pie for you," was all Emily said.

When the parlor door closed behind them, Jim turned up the flame in the big oil-lamp, as Toby removed lumpy dark cloth bag from under his jacket. "I have Knightley's coup-counting shirt and some other odd things from the small trunk in Knightley's quarters behind the taproom. There is a large crowd there tonight," Toby added. "I have not been observed. By the way that the firewater is poured there tonight, no one should see me when I return and likely not remember in the morning if they do."

"There are two ships newly-arrived," Jeremiah nodded. "And the sailors have been permitted leave to carouse."

"So, let us see what Jon Knightley so prized," Elisha Reade looked over his reading glasses, as Jim spread out first the ragged shirt, against which he had tested his revolvers in the afternoon, and then the checkered blue and white calico. He arranged both shirts silently under the lamplight so that the holed elements were in the brightest part of the light.

"There they are, Pa," he said at last. From a drawer in the parlor table, he took the magnifying glass that his mother most often used to examine her embroidery patterns. "Use this and look at the edges of the holes. First in Knightley's shirt; then in that old one of yours that I shot holes in for comparison. Observe the difference."

"Oh, my yes," Elisha exclaimed after a short but exacting comparison. "Congratulations, my boy! I never would have seen it. Mr. Clarke; would you confirm? To preserve your independency of judgment, I will not enlarge on my own observation."

Jeremiah took a few moments longer with the magnifying glass. When he put it aside, his countenance was solemn; he said, "The difference is unmistakable. How do you suppose he did it, James?"

"Beforehand," Jim sighed; it was depressing to be confronted with yet another bit of evidence suggesting a man's general depravity and talent for brutal calculation. "With a pair of sharp scissors, a bit of forethought, and a knowledge of the latest Mrs. Knightleys' impatient temper once her fortune had been spent. Only a matter of time, I suspect. Brother – what are the other items that you have brought us."

"This," Toby brought out from the bag, a small lidded box, about eight inches square and three inches deep; the wood was polished, a rich mahogany color. It opened with a small brass key on a tassel of silk.

"An artists' box of water-colors," Jeremiah Clarke confirmed. "A rather nice one, too. See the tiny porcelain palettes for mixing colors, and the little glass basin for water, and all the pressed blocks of colors? Were we not told that a previous Mrs. Knightley had drowned while painting by the waterside?"

"We were, indeed," Jim nodded. "And the other?" He closed the lid of the paint-box, noting that it bore a little brass plaque with the initials "MKK" engraved in flowing letters above the lock plate. Toby took out another item from the bag; a smaller object than the paint-box, about the size of a five-dollar American coin; a broach, with two colors of hair woven together under a crystal lens, framed in gold and tiny pearls.

"A wedding memento," Elijah Reade nodded. "Look – there is the date, and the initials of the happy couple. There was quite the fashion for this kind of wedding jewelry back east."

"From the Knoxville wife, perhaps." Jim ventured, and Toby nodded. "Perhaps. But there was more in the trunk. I have brought all that I found there. He counted coup against many women."

The other three men were shaken to silence when Toby emptied the rest of the bag contents on the parlor table beside the shirt; a fine lawn handkerchief trimmed with delicate lace, a gold spiral bracelet with a delicate clasp, a finely-carved cameo broach, a single glove to fit a woman's hand, among a jumble of similar items. Jeremiah, as pale as death with horror at the implications, spoke first.

"Does every one of these signify a dead woman? My god, gentlemen, we spoke jestingly of a Bluebeard among us, but never imagined that it could be possible. Mr. Reade, what is your judgment of the situation we have seen unfold before our very eyes?"

Elisha Reade sighed, deep and heartfelt. "I do not know at this point, gentleman. I must confer on the morrow with the authorities. It is plain to me and will be plain to them that Jon Knightley contrived to murder his wife by cutting a small hole in his shirt and claiming that she attacked him first. That any such hole made by firing a bullet into it at close range would have a narrow scorched edge … that was a thing never observed or considered by the sheriff, the judge, the good men of the jury, or even myself, as his defense council. Such knowledge would have changed the entire landscape of the case. Gentlemen, I must ponder this new situation. It is clear to me that Jon Knightley contrived the murder of his wife Martha, here in Galveston. But the evidence of his own vile collection suggests that he has taken advantage of and perhaps murdered other women. In the meantime," Elisha Reade turned his eyes toward Jim and Toby. "Mr. Shaw must return what he has shown to us without suspicion arising."

"I'd rather that he spends a sleepless night," Jeremiah Clarke sounded as if he were grinding his teeth. "The man is a monster, a monster with a smiling, gilded mask. He should know that we suspect him of the vilest of crimes!"

"Ah, but what if he takes the opportunity to gather his valuables and flee to another locality?" Jim said. "He may even take another name and continue murdering wives with impunity? Would you want that on your conscience? I think that we should take my father's advice, and walk warily, allowing Knightley to continue unworried, until the trap of the law closes about him."

"Indeed, James," Elisha appeared relieved. "We may be able to build a solid case against him, having the evidence relating to the deaths of his known wives; the ladies in Natchez and Knoxville. Wait, I beg you all, until we have the evidence of my correspondents there. We must construct a sure and certain trap, in older to capture and hold a monster of this magnitude. Take this collection of sad relics, Mr. Shaw, and return them where they were found. Be assured, gentleman; Jon Knightley will not escape justice. Those mills may grind exasperatingly slow, they do grind fine … and the guilty are caught in them in the end."

Toby silently gathered up the collection of feminine articles and restored them to the bag. He pulled the front of his coat around the small bundle that it made and went like a ghost from the room, leaving Jim, his father and Jeremiah alone with their troubled thoughts.

"I will begin writing letters in the morning, after I speak with the judge and the sheriff of what we have discovered, and of our suspicions. If you would accompany me, James – to impress upon them the gravity of the matter."

"I will draft as many letters as you wish," Jeremiah agreed. "Requesting information regarding Mr. Knightley's activities in various localities. I will begin tonight – for I dare venture that I will not be able to sleep."

"In the meantime, let us rejoin the ladies," Elisha Reade made an effort at resuming a cheerful countenance. "They should not be put to worry over this distressing matter, eh?"

"I wouldn't concern myself overmuch, Pa," Jim answered. "Ma and Rebecca were both pretty shrewd about judging the base nature of the man. I should think they will not be surprised in the least to know that he is a cold-blooded murderer. Indeed, I am certain they both suspected the worst of him in any case."

Late in the evening, as Jim was about to blow out the candle which lighted the guest chamber which he shared with Toby, a light step on the verandah and a gust of a breeze from the Gulf as the French door to the outside heralded Toby's silent return.

"It is done," Toby reported, before Jim could even ask. "They are returned, and no one should be the wiser, as I went in through the opened window without being seen, and took care to place everything as it was before within the trunk."

"I remember now, that is one of your talents," Jim replied, heartened, and reassured. He had been worried that Toby might be taken for a housebreaker, a sneak-thief, and punished out of hand by an angry mob of Knightley's customers, just as an Indian, a foreigner, or a free Negro might well be.

Toby grinned. "I said once before, James; when I have seen a thing, I may call it to mind, exactly as it is, in every detail. Knightley will find nothing of his coup-tokens out of place, or find anything amiss." Inconsequentially, he added, "There was a great noise in the taproom; many voices shouting in anger. I know not over what matter."

"Providing you a convenient distraction," Jim yawned. "Your good fortune that it kept prying eyes from the back of the Knightley place."

***

The following morning, Jim and his father, with Toby and Jeremiah Clarke dined hastily; coffee hot and steaming, on scrambled eggs and Fat Nella's beaten biscuits warm from the oven and dripping with melted butter and honey.

"At the office," Elisha directed, when they set off toward the Strand, huddled against the chill morning air in coats and mufflers, "Begin with writing letters, Jeremiah. I will supply you the addresses when James and I return. What is this, so very early in the morning?"

For a small crowd approached them, surrounding a small wagon drawn by a single horse. The leaden pall of morning fog surrounded them as if in a shroud, the condensation bedewing and dripping like tears, for the form laid in the bed of the wagon; a man-shaped form covered in a dark cloth. Several overcoats, Jim noted. Only his booted feet showed.

"What is the meaning of this?" He demanded of the wagon-driver. "What has happened here? I ask as an agent of the nation of Texas."

"No fear, sir," replied man sitting next to the driver; a man in the solemn black garb of an undertaker – Mr. Turlock, who kept a discrete business a little way farther down the Strand. "It was a duel, honest-fought. Pistols for two at dawn, breakfast for one."

"There are laws prohibiting dueling!" Jim exclaimed, and the driver of the wagon laughed, hawked up and spit into the street with

93

great good humor. "God help you sir, so there are, but a man is bound to defend his honor!"

"Such as it be," Jim murmured, under his breath, for he and Jack both took a dim view of dueling. There were too many other efficient means of getting killed in Texas.

"So, who is the unfortunate loser in this affair, Mr. Turlock?" His father asked, "Any one whom I might know?"

Mr. Turlock chuckled in unprofessional amusement. "As it happens, a man well-known to you: your client, Mr. Knightley!"

"Knightley?" Elisha Reade went pale with horror. "Is this a jest – what has happened? Who was the other in this matter of honor? Bless my soul, we were … that is, there was a matter concerning him that we were…"

"It is, and I make no jest," Mr. Turlock leaned over the back of the wagon seat and twitched the topmost overcoat from be face of the corpse. Toby and Jeremiah were closest to the wagon.

"Yes, that is him, all right," Jeremiah said, and Toby nodded in silent agreement. Elisha Reade was wrung his hands in distress. "My client! What happened? Tell us true if you know, Mr. Turlock. I cannot say that we were friends in any sense, but he was my client, and lately has been in my mind and concern."

"A sturdy young chap came to the tavern last night," Mr. Turlock pulled the covering back over that still, cold face in a businesslike manner. "After a drink or so, he said he was the brother of the late Mrs. Knightley, just returned from a mercantile expedition to Santa Fe. He accused Jon Knightley of murdering his sister in cold blood and of having murdered another wife before that. Well, what could a man do, after being accused in his own place of business in front of witnesses? I daresay that Knightley didn't have his heart in the matter. If it weren't for blustering fools too full of drink, I'd have a lot less casual business, but hey, I'd never thought that he was one of them. A calculating man; a cold fish, if you take my meaning, gentlemen. Wouldn't take any agreement to settle amicably, insisted on his right to challenge, claiming it was a slur on his honor, although I don't think he was over-eager for the encounter. The challenger was one of those reckless young pups with too much liquor in him. Knightley's second could have been talked down from his high horse readily enough, I am thinking," Mr. Turlock shook his head in sad disapproval. "But he didn't, and there he lies, for his pains. The young pup was a better shot, for all that. Must be from being in the Santa Fe trade, I am thinking. Well, I reckon I should plant him next to his missus, then."

"Any open plot will do," Jim replied. "I don't think that Mrs. Knightley will rest all that peacefully next to her late spouse, if it comes to that."

"No, I reckon not," Mr. Turlock grinned, strangely cheerful for an undertaker. "On reconsideration ... I suppose there will be a good turnout for the obsequies in any case."

"He did keep a good house," Elisha Reade admitted.

"But he couldn't keep a good wife," Jim murmured, under his breath. "Not alive and not for long. I presume, Pa, that our project is done?"

"I suppose so," Elisha Reade replied, as Mr. Turlock's driver snapped the reins over his single horse. "I will still pursue it, my boy; not with the same urgency, of course, since there is no longer a life imperiled by matrimony. But justice demands – nay, the blood of these poor murdered women cries from the ground – that their murderer be revealed on this earth for what he was, even as he stands before his creator!"

"Pa, don't fret yourself," Jim begged, for his father still appeared distraught over a matter for which he truly had no knowledge or control. "The matter is finished. Jon Knightley stands before the final judge; it may not have come about in the manner that suits our earthly courts, but I am certain that justice will be done."

"I suppose, son," the elder Reade admitted. "But I will still pursue, knowing that some comfort may come about for the families of those women so wretchedly murdered by that scoundrel. It is only right and just to offer them that knowledge, no matter how late it comes. And I have always sought that which was right and just."

"And so have I," Jim agreed. Silently, Toby nodded agreement, as the clip-clopping of Mr. Turlock's horse faded with distance, even as the morning mist veiled it from sight.

4 – Three Learned Men of Science
The Fourth Adventure

Wherein Jim and Toby are tasked with keeping three scientific emissaries from Prince Frederick of Prussia out of trouble!

"I have just gotten a letter from the president's office, boys," Jack Hays announced, on the afternoon that Jim and Toby returned from sorting out the murderous business of the Yoakum establishment at Pine Bayou. "So, don't get too comfortable. In a couple of days, you must set out and meet a party of gentlemen at Copano and be their escort for the time that they are in Texas – no matter how long they choose to stay, or where they choose to go."

"What does Dr. Jones have for us this time, Jack? And why do these gentlemen need the tender offices of your stiletto-men as wet-nurses?" Jim Reade hung his hat on one of the set of pegs by the door, and dropped into the nearest battered leather chair. Toby, hatless, settled with a barely-stifled groan of exhaustion onto the bearskin hearth-rug. The return from Pine Bayou had been broken by a short stay in Galveston, where Mrs. Reade had plied the two with the best food that her cook, Fat Nella, had to offer, and the very worst that she concocted with her own hands as a demonstration of affection for her son and his blood-brother.

"Because these gentlemen are foreigners, for one," Jack chuckled. "And scientific representatives of his most royal highness Prince Frederick William of Prussia, who according to Dr. Jones, intends to invest in Texas, through the medium of a consortium of noblemen. But before he sinks his noble cash in the venture, the Prince has sent three of his scientific advisors to survey the lay of the land, as it were. They will arrive with their retinue soon in Galveston, and come by coastal sloop to Copano to begin their survey."

"We could have just stayed in Galveston and met them at the docks," Jim stifled a yawn. Yes, and prolonged the stay with his parents, although he didn't think he could endure much more of his mother's disastrous attempts at baking turnovers, sweet biscuits, and cakes.

"Indeed, but I did not know of their arrival before three days ago," Jack unfolded the letter and spoke in his most reasonable and heartening tones. "And you can take a few days – but no more than three – before meeting these scientific gentlemen. You will know them, because they will be foreigners, of course. My orders are that you should accompany them where they wish to go and to keep them from serious trouble. There is money for the Republic involved – a thing that we are desperately short of – if they produce a favorable report."

"Yes, we haven't been paid in money in months," Toby contributed from his comfortable position on the hearth-rug. "Over and above our expenses. Not that I keep count of your white-man conventions."

"At some point, all accounts will be squared," Jack replied, ignoring the snort of skeptical derision from the hearth-rug. "As men of intelligent creativity, I know that you can manage it. Prince Frederick William or his secretary, was thoughtful enough to send their names and qualifications in his letter to Dr. Jones."

"Give it to us now," Jim sighed. "So that we can become accustomed to the notion of being bear-leaders to the servants of a foreign prince."

"All right, then," Jack's grin broadened. "The senior of our scientific trio is the eminent botanist, Herr Professor Manfred von Brockdorff, who rejoices in the title of Graf von Brockdorff. The equally eminent geologist Dietmar Kraus is not a noble – a mere professor. And Herr Doctor Theodore Maier is a real medical doctor and surgeon, seconded from service with the Prussian army."

"Well … they sound like a much better class of folk than the Yoakums," Jim remarked, after taking all this in. "And they can't possibly be any more difficult than thieves, murderers, and dog-stealers."

"We would hope, brother," Toby answered, but not as if he really had any real conviction.

***

A week later, the coastal sloop *Eliza* arrived and tied up at one of the three wharves at Copano. Jim and Toby had brought three extra horses and a pair of pack mules, staying in the house of Joseph Plummer while they waited the arrival of the *Eliza*. There was much excitement among the regular residents of the tiny hamlet, upon hearing that Jim and Toby were there to escort some important foreign visitors.

"A titled gentleman, you don't say?" exclaimed the Widow Jackson, a handsome matron of about forty, who kept a tiny boarding establishment in her cottage of shell concrete, which had a view of Copano Bay from a garden planted thick with flowering cosmos, potatoes, and herbs. "Well, I never!"

"You would if he offered, like a gentleman," Joe Plummer added with a leer and the Widow Jackson ruffled like an angry hen, told him to keep a civil tongue in his head and flounced away to speak to Mrs. Plummer, although she cast indignant glances over her shoulder now and again.

Joe Plummer chuckled coarsely, and remarked in a lower voice, "Becky Jackson is tired of the single life, and on the prowl for another husband. I'd say beware, but you two fellows are a mite young for her taste. She wants an older man, one with a sizable … property and a solid profession. Better tell your foreign fellows to steer clear, or she'll catch them in her man-trap before you can blink."

Toby and Jim exchanged glances; Toby's expression one of amusement, and Jim's of mild horror. "It might not be so bad," Toby ventured, in judicial consideration. "Is she a good cook?"

"One of the best, I'd have to admit," Joe Plummer admitted. "And pleasant-tempered, mostly. Her last husband, old Ezra Jackson, had a good appetite for her vittles; everyone at his funeral say he was laid out with a smile on his face and a gut almost too big for the coffin."

***

But there was no smile on the faces of anyone, when the *Eliza* tied up, that afternoon. And as far as Jim could see, the deck was piled high with bundles, crates, and trunks – surely too much for the five men who strode off the sloop as soon as the gangplank was secured. There was a sixth man also – who seemed to be giving directions to the sailors and deckhands ready to unload the sloop.

"We may need more than two mules, brother," Toby whispered. "If all that is theirs – and I do not see any other passengers."

"We'll work out something," Jim murmured in an aside, as three men were in hearing distance and bearing down, with the other two lurking in the background. Those two – young, fit, and under arms had a soldierly bearing about them. Jim rather wished that he had brought some of the other stiletto-men with him, even someone like Creed Taylor or Albert Biddle. Jack himself would have been a solid addition to the reception committee. Instead, he braced his shoulders and addressed his remarks to the tallest and most important-appearing of the gentlemen bearing down upon him.

"If I am addressing the Graf von Brockdorff, I welcome you again to Texas, sir. Jim Reade, Esquire, and Toby Shaw of the Delaware Nation. We have been sent by my commander, Captain Hays and President Anson Jones of the Republic of Texas to assist you as might be needed…"

"Reade?" the gentleman demanded; a burly and choleric sort, with a countenance scarred with several straight slashes which suggested he had fought with bladed weapons on a regular basis. "Hah – are those all the horses you have brought? Clearly, we will need more than that. Brockdorff, at your service." He crushed Jim's hand, nodded briskly toward Toby, who was doing his best to be at one with the immediate surroundings. "We will require a place to stay, while our belongings are unloaded. My servant Achterberg will see to that. My compatriots; Professor Kraus, Doctor Meier … Achterberg!" he bellowed over his shoulder, and Jim started. That was an authoritative and noble bellow if he had ever heard one. "Fuchs! Haun! Attend!"

The other gentlemen of science stood half a pace back at Brockdorff's elbow, and Jim was aware of a sinking feeling as he introduced himself.

"Maier," said the first; a thin and youngish man, but wearing thick glasses, which magnified watery blue eyes.

"Certainly," Jim replied. A medical doctor, and a near-sighted one. Well – this would turn out well.

"Herr Professor Kraus," announced the third man, in an over-loud voice. He was of middle-age, slender and lanky. His handshake was strong, his fingers callused like a working man's. "I am greatly anticipating the pleasure of exploring the particular geology of your sedimentary formations." A heavy coat hung on him like clothing on a scarecrow, the pockets of it weighted down with heavy objects. One of them, Jim noticed, was a large hearing trumpet. "Pleased," Jim replied, wondering if this meant that Professor Kraus meant that he was going to search Jim's coat pockets or something

"You will have to speak up," Professor Maier said, when Jim introduced himself to the professor. "Kraus is very hard of hearing."

"Never eat herring, gives me gas," Professor Kraus announced. "Please to meet you, young man, although I didn't catch your name. Where then are we to stay, Brockdorff, while our supplies and equipment are being unloaded?"

"We have made arrangements for your party at the boarding house of Mrs. Jackson – a very respectable widow," Jim replied; as hers was the only house with sufficient room for guests to sleep in beds, rather than in a pallet on the floor of the verandah. "We did not expect … such a large party, sirs."

"Avoid parties," Professor Kraus grunted. "Waste of time, flouncing around when I have work to do."

"We reduced our necessary entourage to the minimum," von Brockdorff replied, vaguely perplexed. "Only Achterberg and the two soldiers as guards."

Twice as many has had been expected, Jim thought – although Jack had said something about an entourage. He had definitely not mentioned the steadily growing pile of trunks, crates and bales. A scientific expedition; and he would have thought that such would have started with little, and concluded with much. As it was, this expedition was commencing with much, and what it would conclude with was anyone's guess.

"We'll make arrangements," Jim answered, determinedly cheerful, although he murmured in an aside to Toby, "We'll have to hire a wagon and teams, then. Who in Copano has such for hire?"

***

"Why, bless my soul – I do!" exclaimed a beaming Widow Jackson. "And my son, young Corb to drive it! I'm sure we can come to some proper arrangement – you leave that to me, young Mister Reade. Oh, my stars!" she looked down from the gate. "These furriner gents don't travel light, do they? I'll have to rustle up a place for them sojers of theirs to sleep." She bustled away, leaving Jim and Toby to look at each other.

"That is one thing accomplished then, James." Toby ventured. "So – have we any sense of where the gentlemen wish to travel?"

"North to the frontier," Jim sighed. "And then east as far as the pine woods, then down the Brazos toward Galveston. It's to be a wandering journey, allowing them to survey the land and make collections of plants and what-not. Von Brockdorff is also an accomplished artist and draftsman; he says he is to make a detailed record to guide Prince Frederick William and his friends. They plan a leisurely two or three months at this. I had better start drafting my first report to Jack and let him know the plan."

When the party departed Copano, some days later, it was as a vastly more expansive one than originally expected; one large wagon, loaded to the point where the axles groaned warningly and pulled by three teams of bullocks, a small train of pack mules, and the men of the party, all on horseback and the Widow Jackson, riding primly astride and holding a parasol over her head as she rode. On the strength of her cooking, and a stated willingness to work with von Brockdorff's servant, Mr. Achterberg, she had been hired as cook for the party, leaving the boarding house in the charge of her two older children.

"So which one has she got her sights on, Reade?" Joe Plummer offered a lewd wink on the morning of their departure. "The count, the professor or the doctor?"

"I have no idea," Jim replied, glumly thinking that this whole mission increasingly resembled a circus. Brockdorff's expedition included four canvas tents; the largest of them serving as his sleeping quarters, dining room and office. All these temporary canvas quarters were fitted with folding camp furniture and every portable convenience imaginable. All they needed was a tame lion and a trapeze artist.

Still, against his gloomy expectations, the first few weeks went well; extraordinary well, according to von Brockdorff.

"His Highness will be most pleased," von Brockdorff's usual gruffness had mellowed slightly, by the time they reached the town of Victoria. Jim wondered how much of that mellowing could be accounted for by the quality of the Widow Jackson's cooking, or that they had encountered nothing but fair weather since departing Copano. The sun shown in a faultlessly azure sky, pleasingly dotted with drifts of pure white cloud; the countryside dotted with sweeps of wildflowers, spread like a marvelous quilt between stands of noble oaks and thickets of tall reeds. Nothing disrupted the work of the three gentlemen of science; von Brockdorff collected flower and leaf specimens, pressing and drying some, sketching others in detailed water-colors, while Professor Kraus prowled with a little hammer, collecting up pebbles and chipping slivers off larger rocks. Doctor Maier, whose interests also included weather phenomenon, solemnly took temperature and barometric readings at regular intervals.

"I can't think of any good this all does, in the long run," Jim confessed to Toby and the two German soldiers who accompanied the party. "But it keeps them happy and contented, and out of trouble."

"Oh, *ya*," nodded Private Haun. He was the taller and more voluble of the two; a small head on a long neck and narrow shoulders. It amused Jim to be told that '*haun*' meant 'rooster' in German. Private Fuchs, on the other hand, was short, and red-haired, with narrow features and slightly beady eyes. '*Fuchs*' meant 'fox' – further reason for amusement. Jim wondered if the two had been deliberately chosen for this detail because of their names. "So – Jeem; you think we see Indians?"

"You've already seen Indians," Jim replied. "Mr. Shaw." Both soldiers looked skeptical in the extreme. They had obviously expected moccasins, loincloth, and feathers, but Toby affected ordinary clothing these days; only his long braids and the star-iron talisman hung on a buckskin thong from his neck hinted at his Delaware origins.

"*Ya*, but real wild Indians – like the Comanche," Private Haun looked wistful.

"You better hope you never see a wild Comanche," Jim answered. "They'll cut your throat and take your hair by way of saying hello."

***

The first trouble found them in Victoria, to Jim's dismay; not delivered to the peppery-tempered and autocratic von Brockdorff – but instead to Professor Kraus. Whom, aside from failing to fully grasp most of what was said to him with or without the aid of his ear-trumpet, was a relatively inoffensive little man, and married already which removed him from being the main prize in the Widow Jackson's marital stakes. The doctor was only a little older than Jim, who if he had been a betting man, would have staked his money on Brockdorff and the appeal of the noble title.

That trouble came upon them in the main street, in the heat of the day, as they waited impatiently outside of the largest general store in Victoria, while the Widow Jackson completed the purchase of some early summer ripe melons, a pyramid of which were stacked before the general store windows. A sudden sharp gust of wind sent the dust flying, along with dead leaves and torn merchant circulars – and one especially fine straw planter's hat, whisked from the head of a stout, red-faced party in a fancy flowered waistcoat and under the hooves of Professor Kraus's horse. The horse, understandably startled and shied sideways, taking Professor Kraus out of his disjointed conversation with von Brockdorff. One hoof came down upon the hat with a sound of someone crunching celery, and Professor Kraus loosed a flood of exotic curse-words... or at least, Jim assumed they were curse-words.

Meanwhile, the owner of the hat – considerably the worse for having been crushed by a horse – elbowed his way past Jim and the

107

two soldiers, Haun and Fuchs and roared, "Damn your eyes, look at what you've done to my hat!"

Professor Kraus looked down from horseback and replied, "Fat? My good sir, you are obese and choleric and that's my judgment as a man of science."

"What did you just call me!" demanded the man in the flowered waistcoat. "You are called out, sah! I demand satisfaction for the insult – or you are no gentleman!"

"*Unglaublich*!" Professor Kraus drew himself up, temporarily devoid of his English. "There was no insult or offense intended! I merely …"

"He's a foreign fellow," Jim elbowed his way in between Professor Kraus and his incensed challenger. "Really. And he's doing important research, very important research. For the Prince of Prussia. He meant no offense. A simple apology would…"

"I don't care if he's working for the High Panjandrum or the King of Persia!" the offended man roared, while Professor Kraus shouted, "Apologize? For what, I ask of you?"

"He wants to fight you in a duel!" Jim shouted into the hearing trumpet. Professor Kraus sputtered in astonishment. "Ridiculous! Why should I fight a duel?"

"Because you've been challenged?" Jim replied. "It's the custom…"

"Custard? I don't see any custard," Professor Kraus answered. "Stuff's for milksops and children anyway. This fellow is fat, and if he can't see that in the mirror, then I suggest that his eyesight is defective as well!"

"That's enough!" roared the doctor's challenger, now turning an even deeper shade of puce. "Name your weapon, sir! And your second – and the time! Knox – sir, you are my second!"

"Her name is Winifred, not that it is any concern of yours," Professor Kraus replied, and von Brockdorff shouted into the hearing trumpet, "Your weapon, Kraus – to fight a duel with! As the challenged, you have the right to name the weapon that you will fight him with!"

"I already said that her name is Winifred!" Professor Kraus barked, while Jim and von Brockdorff exchanged frustrated glances. The man named Knox, a lanky man in the rough and slightly less ornamental clothing of a blacksmith lurked at his friend's elbow – as near as Jim could hear, he was trying to dissuade his friend from fighting a duel.

"Looky here, Boone; there's no call for getting all het-up. It was an accident, sure enough, I seen it with my own eyes." Herr Doctor Maier produced the little book in which he jotted his scientific findings, and wrote in it before passing it to the Professor, upon whom a measure of understanding finally dawned.

"Hah! A duel, is it? Then you shall have satisfaction!"

"Gentlemen, the practice of dueling is against the law!" Jim shouted, hoping to gain attention, now that Professor Kraus had grasped the concept. "Participating in or abetting a duel will result in charges being brought against all parties."

"But I have been challenged!" Professor Kraus swung down from his saddle, eye to eye with his prospective adversary, and unexpectedly assured in the face of this challenge. "And I have the choice of weapons, *hein*? And to choose the time of my convenience and the place?"

"Of course!" his challenger was now the bright-red of a chicken wattle, glared ferociously at Professor Kraus, ignoring the low-voiced comment from his friend and drafted second. At that very moment, the Widow Jackson came running from the general store, clasping her hands to her quite substantial bosoms, pleading, "Oh, Professor – you must not … you cannot! You are a man of science and learning!"

"Nevertheless, madam, I have been challenged," Professor Kraus returned. By some miracle, he comprehended every word, exactly. Jim briefly entertained the suspicion that perhaps the professor derived amusement from deliberately miss-hearing what was said to him, especially things which he did not want to hear. "It is the custom of Prussian gentlemen to respond in such a case. The time for our appointment is now," he continued, directing his remarks to his challenger. "The place is here – and my second," he cast a glance sideways toward von Brockdorff, "Is the Graff von Brockdorff, who has given satisfaction on the field on many occasions. Graff, if you will oblige?"

"Of course!" and von Brockdorff assumed a marital posture at Professor Kraus's elbow, supremely oblivious to Jim's horrified protests and the Widow Jackson's tears. "Your chosen weapon, Herr Professor!"

"Melons," Professor Kraus smiled, beatifically. "Two of them, at a space of five paces. If you would oblige me, Frau Jackson, my purse is yours, for purchasing the required ammunition."

"What?" von Brockdorff was shaken entirely out of countenance, mirrored by the horror and disbelief on the choleric countenance of the owner of the crushed hat. "You cannot be serious, Herr Professor – this is a ridiculous perversion of all that is honorable… a…"

"It is a ridiculous challenge," Professor Kraus returned. "Yet I have every intention of going through with it … on my terms. It is my right, is it not, as the challenged party?"

"He has him there," commented Fuchs, over Jim's shoulder, while the Widow Jackson hurried back to the store, her son in her wake. Meanwhile, the affronted owner of the crushed hat recovered his voice and bearing. "This is a mockery!" he stormed. "A mockery of a serious challenge made in earnest! No, don't try and talk me down, Dixon – the insult is unforgivable!"

"A challenge which you made in an impetuous spirit, knowing that such duels are without the law," Jim pointed out, in a studiedly neutral voice, and the man in blacksmith's apron – Dixon – shot him an approving glance. "A matter easy to be angered by and the gentleman is within his rights, as these things go, in making a choice regarding the weapon. But as a representative of our nation showing hospitality to guests, I would suggest that apologies be exchanged, in a calm and reasonable manner. To go through with this ridiculous contest will only make you the laughing-stock of Victoria. Perhaps Professor Kraus, too, but he is a foreigner, and will be gone from here in days."

"It is also customary," Doctor Maier pointed out in judicious tones, as he blinked through his thick glasses, "In these affairs of honor, for the seconds to attempt a reconciliation."

"It's the plain truth of it, Boone," Dixon said, in soothing tones. "'Hit's an honest thing to do. Y' don't want to be the laughing-stock of Victoria – fighting a duel with them melons, over a busted hat and a plain misunderstanding? Tell ya plain, if y' go through with it, they'll be telling the story long after yer dead and buried, no matter which of yer wins."

Mr. Achterberg, bland and anonymous as always, sounded as if he were murmuring the same sentiments in German to his liege lord, which Jim noted with relief; another ally in the effort to cool things down. Herr Professor Kraus was listening intently through his hearing trumpet, although he gave every evidence of being eager to lob melons at the space of five feet. Jim had to admit to himself that it would be a tall comic tale for the ages; Jack would likely see the humor, but President Jones would not, and Prince Frederick William would be stupendously unamused. Toby was not much of a help; he was leaning against the Jackson wagon, with an expression his normally impassive face which suggested he was quite eager to witness pair of white men contesting to fling melons at each other. The whole matter teetered on the brink for the space of two or three breaths, before Mr. Boone let out a sigh which expanded and then deflated his fancy waistcoat by several degrees, and extended his right hand, humbled to be courteous.

"I reckon you got the right of it, gentlemen; all of you. I withdraw my challenge on receipt of an apology. I admit that I got a mite carried away. It was a new hat, barely broken in."

"I am indeed most sorry for the accident," Professor Kraus dignity was unassailable, yet Jim also noted that appeared vaguely disappointed. "I had no deliberate intent for my horse to crush your very elegant and functional hat. And I withdraw my subsequent comments made concerning your person. I was carried away by emotion."

"Apology accepted, sir!" The two shook hands; everyone but Toby appeared relieved. "But I wanted to see two white men throw melons at each other," He murmured quietly to Jim. "Or potatoes. Potatoes would have been even better." Jim made a mental note to enlighten his blood-brother regarding how what could have been an epic disaster had just been averted. Toby certainly understood the concept of two men taking up arms against each other over an insult, but clearly not some of the finer details of the *code duello*.

***

Mr. Boone, the peppery gentleman with the damaged hat was invited to join them for supper that afternoon, a supper expertly cooked by the Widow Jackson and served by Mr. Achterberg; that and several rounds of very good French brandy provided from the Graff's limitless stores, smoothed and soothed any remaining bad feeling over the matter among the company. But Jim could not let himself relax entirely. The weeks ahead of him, escorting the jaunt of the three gentlemen of science held plenty of potential for disaster. Professor Kraus, backed by von Brockdorff voiced a desire to travel deep into the highlands, the hilly country north of San Antonio, that line of hills that lined the horizon like a vast escarpment. Jim was in two minds about that; but since he and Toby had the friendship of Old Owl, Mopechucope of the Penateka, and von Brockdorff's retinue did include the soldiers Haun and Fuchs and a fair quantity of weaponry among their stores, he approved the Professor's plans.

"No farther than the old San Saba fort," he conceded. "The Llano and the upper Colorado are Comanche hunting grounds. We have good friends among some, but the others are … not inclined to be overly-understanding."

"Real Comanche!" Fuchs exclaimed in delight, while Haun chimed in, just as eagerly. Jim sighed. Nothing he could say would convince him that the average Comanche warrior was a brutal, treacherous, slave-taker, out for anything they could loot without going through much trouble about it; although he did have to admit that Mopechucope had truly proved a man of his word. Whatever pagan magic he had worked to protect Jim and Toby on the occasion of their first encounter had proved strong and true – as strong and true as his pledge of friendship.

They left San Antonio behind early in spring and moved by gradual steps into the limestone hills; green and dotted with magnificent stands of oak trees, at which their guests all marveled – and at the spreading fields grown with wildflowers in bloom; acres of blue buffalo clover, pink primrose, gold and red Mexican Hat, and purple verbena. Von Brockdorff was afire with artistic energy; painting and map-drawing with increasing vigor and delight. The Widow Jackson fetched him representative samples and plants, telling him of their names, frontier lore, and various properties, in between her duties over the cook-fire. She appeared to be a considerable repository of herb-wife lore. Jim, seeing this developing association, thought in resignation it was likely that the Widow Jackson had selected her next husband. He gloomily wondered how that would rebound at the court of a foreign prince; a royal scientific advisor turning up with a foreign bride. Whatever plans the royal prince had for Texas would likely sink over it. He couldn't imagine the Widow Jackson – blunt-spoken, middle-aged, and frontier-capable – as a wild success at a noble court in Europe.

Over a small fire, a little aside from the main camp, he consulted with his blood-brother; who as he had feared, did not seem worried over the implications.

"She's a spirited woman, James," Toby shrugged. "I don't know why you worry. Among my people, a woman like that would be a prize for an older warrior. She is still pleasing to look upon, a good cook, her children are grown, her lodge a comfortable one. And her talk makes him laugh. He could do worse, Brother. He's of an age where he has probably seen many pretty young women looking with longing eyes at him, yet have no skill or conversation worth finding to his appeal. Do not worry, my brother. The Great Spirit has all things in hand, whatever we may wish."

"Your words wafted toward your Great Spirits' ear!" Jim answered. Since no one else seemed worried about the Widow Jackson and her unabashed pursuit of the Graff von Brockdorff, he put his concerns aside, concluding that since von Brockdorff was a man of experience and maturity he ought to be able to look after himself when it came to a matrimonially-determined woman.

***

Up into the distant hill country they journeyed, farther and farther from the settled frontier, past the little towns, fortified homesteads and stockades established by extended families, from which the men of the colony went every day to tend their fields, their flocks and herds. They went even beyond those few scattered outposts, into the edge of the grasslands beyond the hills – the proper borders of Comancheria, the domain of the warrior horse-lords of the southern plains, setting up camp, in a meadow by where the river made a deep pool in a lazy bend, where they intended to remain for a few weeks.

They did encounter a few scattered hunters; and once a substantial band of Mopechucope's people, the Penateka Comanche; a party of mostly men, lightly burdened. All, even that band parlayed willingly with Toby, claiming they were hunters, although Jim thought it most likely they were heading into the Nueces Strip, or raid into Mexico for horses and whatever other unconsidered trifles they could collect. Von Brockdorff, Doctor Maier and Professor Kraus were no less enthralled with these scattered encounters than Haun and Fuchs.

"Real wild Indians, at last!" Fuchs exclaimed, admiringly, although Jim did note that the two German soldiers kept their hands on or close to their personal arms during these visits. The Widow Jackson radiated disapproval of these parlays and herself kept her own weapons – a stout long-handled frying pan and a long sharp cooking knife close to hand.

"Heathens!" she muttered under her breath to Jim. "I can't forget the way they sacked and burned Linnville, those red devils almost murdered poor Mrs. Watts! It was only the steel bones in her corset that saved her life. Tried to shoot her full of arrows, they did!" She vanished into the small tent that was her sleeping quarters, still muttering furiously about the perfidy of the Comanche and let the flap of the tent fall too, as another small party of Comanche – this time men and women both, approached the camp.

Word had gotten out, probably whispering among the birds in the sky, about the strange, foreign white men, men possessing powerful medicine. Within a matter of days of establishing a temporary camp upon the banks of the Llano River, they were being visited regularly by Comanche, no less curious about the foreigner wise men than the wise men were concerning the Comanche. Jim took to retiring early to his bed-roll and awaking an hour or so before dawn, so worried was he regarding a lightning-fast, smash and stab raid upon the camp at that hour. But the visitors – all wiry and bronzed from the sun, their hair braided and adorned with beads and feathers, their faces with paint, dressed in crude buckskin mixed with trade cloth and cast-off garments gained through such means as Jim did not want to contemplate – were courteous as their customs allowed, and gradually he relaxed. But not enough to give up the habit of getting up early. Von Brockdorff's drawings seemed to fascinate them most particularly, although the professor's interest in rocks and Doctor Maier's medical kit came in for their due in interest.

"I have the latest and best instruments available in my trunks that we carried along on this expedition," Doctor Maier boasted one day late in spring, while Toby obediently translated to a gaggle of Comanche men and women. "I can alleviate with surgery almost any condition suffered by mankind." The doctor-surgeon carried on with a lecture on what was now medically possible, showing off the contents of the trunk which carried his medical gear, although Jim did not think the intently-listening audience grasped much of it, even in Toby's translation. Until the moment when a very young Indian warrior, little older than a boy, with a thick mane of black hair hanging down his back asked a single question of Toby.

"He asks – can you give a blind man back his sight?" Doctor Maier appeared to consider the matter carefully and with respect to the questioner.

"It would depend upon the cause of blindness," he replied in a guarded fashion. "I could not promise medical success without a careful examination of the sufferer."

Toby relayed that reply to the young Indian, who nodded in an impassive way. He stalked away and leaped onto his horse without a backward look.

"I wonder what that was about?" The Widow Jackson ventured; a question answered the following day at mid-afternoon, when the young Indian returned, accompanied by a half-dozen others; three young men like himself, a young girl of about twelve or so, and an older man, who might have been all of Jim's age of twenty-four, but for the weathering of his face and body, looked ten or twenty years older. It was a hard life, for the horseman-lords of the plains – and one which aged a human body at a tragic rate.

"They say he is blind, Red Knife, the older brother of their father," Toby reported, after a short exchange with the visitors. "And a renowned warrior and taker of horses. Blindness has come on slowly – now he can barely see the sun in the sky."

"Cataracts," Doctor Maier said, after a brief examination of Red Knife. "Very far advanced … but I can do it. It is complicated surgery, of course – with a certain chance of resulting in complete blindness for the patient. But I am completely confident of success."

"You'd better be," Jim warned. "Unhappy Comanches are not content with bad-mouthing you all over town. You'd prolly not escape with your life and hair … or any of the rest of us, either."

"Is that so?" For the first time, Doctor Maier looked somewhat shaken. Both von Brockdorff and Professor Kraus were away from their camp although within the sound of a shout or a gunshot, accompanied by an attentive and well-armed Haun and Fuchs. "Oh, my. It only occurs to me now that I may have over-promised in some small degree. But nevertheless, I must go through with it, now. Departing from here is out of the question, of course. Besides," he straightened the lapels of his dark coat, "I regret the risk that this operation may entail for the party. But I am pledged to aid the sick and injured, no matter of what color, nation, or condition. But there must be certain precautions ..." He continued outlining them to Toby, who relayed certain of them to the hovering group of Comanche men and boys. The girl sat a little aside, patiently waiting; Jim wondered briefly at that, as she did not bear much of a likeness to the others, aside from having black hair and a weather-burned complexion.

Doctor Maier's conditions and preparations for performing the operation were extensive. The others of their party returned from their rock and botanical-sample hunting mid-way through the lecture. Von Brockdorff immediately took out his sketchpad and began limning portraits of the visitors, although the girl quickly ducked her head, and the youngest of the Comanche visitors scowled at him.

At mid-morning on the following day, Doctor Maier directed, and only if there was no wind to blow dust around. He insisted on absolute cleanliness, and set Mr. Achterberg and the Widow Jackson to filling every kettle with clean water to boil over the fire.

"The water to irrigate the eyes must be free of contamination, and cooled to lukewarm," Doctor Maier explained, his pale blue eyes gleaming behind his thick glasses. "And – insects must be kept away. My hands must be steady and my concentration absolute. I will perform this operation in the bright light and open air, since there would be a danger of lamps igniting that ether that I must use to anesthetize my patient … and there must be some bags of sand, or other weights – to hold my patients' head absolutely still during surgery and for a period of recovery."

Doctor Maier went on in this manner for some minutes; Jim assumed that it was because the doctor was one of those obsessed with a subject and just as obsessed with a need to talk about it to anyone who would listen. Which would have been interesting; listening to an expert telling yarns about what they knew best always was. But Jim had little interest and no stomach for hearing about how Red Knife's eyeball would be carefully sliced open and that part of his eye – the part causing his blindness – would be excised. He knew himself not to be a particularly squeamish man, especially not after some of his and Toby's ventures, many of which involved dead bodies. But slicing into a living eye … no, he hastily got up and made conversation with the Widow Jackson, capable and busy with supper preparation over the campfire.

"Is there anything that I can do for you?" he asked, knowing that Mr. Achterberg was usually stuck with the most menial tasks. "In the interests of supper, I mean. I am … curiously disinterested in hearing details of what Doctor Maier is planning …"

"Turns my own stomach, indeed," the Widow Jackson agreed. "If'n you don't mind – can you set a passel of dried apples to soak for me? Emil – that is, Mr. Achterberg has already done the potatoes. I thought that I would make apple pie for the gentlemen tonight. I wonder, are them wild Comanche going to stay for supper? Fair makes my blood run cold, to think on it!"

"From the look of it, they have made their own arrangements," Jim observed. It looked now as if the Comanche were setting up their own campsite and cook-fire, although it appeared that the girl was doing all the work. He was given to understand that was their custom, which accounted for his own observation that most Comanche women appeared like hard-driven drudges, whereas the Lipan and Delaware women of his observation looked more handsome, more like women in command of their destiny, hearth, and home.

"That girl of theirs?" The Widow Jackson broke into his ruminations. "Oh, she's a slave, all right, Mr. Reade; a Meskin, if I have my own eyesight and brain in the proper adjustment. Poor girl – one o' them poor captives, taken so long ago, she's one o' them. They talk a mighty bunch o' how those Injun's live wild an' brave an' free? Never saying anything o' how womenfolk do all the hard work o' it all."

She slammed down the cooking fork, by which Jim grasped that the Widow Jackson was not happy. He bent to the task of pouring hot water over a quantity of leather-like slices of dried apple, and finally thought to reply, "It's a custom. And not one – in the present circumstances – to which we have any cause for objection, even tactfully. Not if we wish to have any desire to escape, with our lives and scalps intact. The water-butt is nearly empty, Mrs. Jackson. Shall I go fetch more?"

"Yes indeedy," the Widow Jackson now looked nearly as frightened as she could ever be. "Mr. Reade, are we truly in that much danger?"

"Not any more than we have been all along," Jim took up a pair of tin pails. "Pray that Doctor Maier's surgery tomorrow is a success beyond all imagining."

***

At mid-morning, when the sun stood high in the sky and the wind barely stirred the rustling leaves overhead or the tall heads of the grasses which grew thickly along the margins of the meadow, Doctor Maier rolled the sleeves of his shirt up to the elbow, and washed his hands one last time.

"We are ready now," he said; at those words, Jim, Toby, and the others took up their assigned positions, armed with palm-frond fans, in a semi-circle around Red Knife, taking care not to block the sunlight falling full upon him. Dr. Maier's patient lay face up on a sturdy camp table covered with a heavy blanket, his sightless eyes falling closed as the ether took effect. A pair of flour sacks half-filled with clean sand braced his head firmly on either side. After careful negotiation through Toby with the other Comanche, Doctor Maier had secured Red Knife's hands, torso, thighs, and feet to the table with lengths of strong cord, explaining that it was absolutely necessary that there be no movement from his patient, voluntary or otherwise. "I begin, now," Doctor Maier took up a peculiarly-shaped small surgical knife, and Jim fixed his eyes on the far horizon. This was all terribly disturbing, but he'd be damned if he would faint like a squeamish girl; Toby would laugh himself silly and the scorn of the Comanche would be unbearable. He kept his gaze fixed on anything other than the unconscious man tied to the table, the sunlight casting brief sparks off Doctor Maier's razor-sharp surgical knife – only on such unwary flies which happened to blunder into the space where the surgery was taking place.

The four young Comanche men also stood with fans in the semi-circle, for which Jim was grateful. This meant that they did not have their hands on weapons, at least for a short space. The young girl remained by their own campfire, going about the business of whatever meant housekeeping for the Comanche. Likely that was rather like what the Widow Jackson was doing for their party, although Jim knew that she had the assistance of her son and Mr. Achterberg and himself, when it came down to it.

It seemed to him like a nervous, vigilant, and sweaty eternity; trying not to watch the doctor's blade, torn between fixing his attention the horizon and on any nearby flies. But the sun had not even reached zenith, when Doctor Maier set aside the knife … and what was that, a needle trailing a wisp of black silk … and announced, "It is finished."

One of the young Comanche – the shrewdest of them – looked from Doctor Maier, to the unconscious patient, and asked a question, which Toby relayed almost as soon as the words were out of his mouth. "Will Uncle be able to see again?"

"We will not know for certain until he awakes, and for several days thereafter," Doctor Maier returned, with dignity. He turned to wash his hands again, in a bowl of water proffered by the Widow Jackson. "He will be able to see; likely not as well as he did before the visual affliction took hold. But I believe that he will be able to see, following my operation."

"Thin assurance, Doctor," Jim murmured, as Toby relayed this information to the Comanche, along with the warning that their uncle must remain laying down and his head absolutely still while healing commenced. The eldest of the young Comanche nodded stiffly and they carried the still-unconscious Red Knife away on a litter made from two lodge-poles and the blanket that he had lain on, with a care which proved they had taken Doctor Maier's admonishments seriously.

***

"When will you know if you have been successful?" Jim asked, doing his level best to sound casual, unworried.

"Three, four days, perhaps," Doctor Maier sounded confident – but Jim suspected darkly that he could speak so because he didn't really have a clue as to the usual temper and conduct of unhappy Comanche on the warpath.

He continued his habit of waking very early in the morning, before the sky in the east paled with the first hint of dawn, pouring a splash of barely-warm coffee from the pot left sitting at the edge of the ashes of last night's cook-fire, and sitting with it, his pair of Colts and his shotgun in a sheltered spot a little apart from their campfire. The morning after Doctor Maier's open-air surgery, a silent shadow ghosted from camp to join him.

"You keep careful watch, my brother," Toby remarked in a whisper. Jim did not startle; he was accustomed to how Toby moved without breaking a fallen twig or brushing against a leafy branch. "You have no trust in the authority of Old Owl?"

"Him I trust," Jim replied. "His fellows? Especially the young ones, and if they bear a resentment? Not especially. It is my fervent prayer that our good Doctor has truly restored the sight of a blind man, and that the age of miracles is not yet over."

"It is not, James," Toby returned, as equable as ever. "The doctor has powerful medicine."

They sat in silence for many minutes, watching the camp and the camp of the Comanches beyond, while the sky lightened imperceptibly in the east. A flash of sparks from the Comanche cook-fire briefly revealed the girl, adding twigs to the fire. In their own camp, the Widow Jackson emerged from the small tent that she shared with her son; bound on the same errand, a dark and skirted shadow against the gradually glowing fire.

"Well, we will die with a good breakfast in the offing, if the man does not regain his sight," Jim remarked, again in a whisper, and Toby chuckled almost noiselessly. "And the Graff with the taste of a good kiss on his lips," Jim added, as another shadow emerged through the flaps of the largest tent which von Brockdorff shared with Achterberg and the other scientific gentleman. The shadow merged in the dark with that of the Widow Jackson, in a brief and passionate embrace. Jim and Toby observed, without comment, as the shadows separated at last.

"It appears that the Widow Jackson has made her choice," Jim said, finally, when the second shadow returned to the tent.

"She will make his lodge a pleasant one," Toby nodded, and Jim wondered if the Widow Jackson would perform that miracle on some drafty stone pile in Prussia.

***

It was not three or four days later – but a mere two, when the young Comanche who had first approached Doctor Maier came to their campfire in the late afternoon. The three gentlemen of science had been holding a conference on how much longer they should remain. Professor Kraus had entirely exhausted the variety of stones in the immediate vicinity and von Brockdorff had sketched and mapped sufficient to fill a bulging portfolio; they were eager to move on and explore fresher horizons. Jim approved enthusiastically of any move which would bring them back to the settled side of the frontier, but the conscientious Doctor Maier wished to linger for a few more days, claiming the best interests of

Red Knife – as well as continue tending to those curious Indian visitors with less-drastic medical needs. Infuriatingly, Toby agreed with him.

"The knife-medicine healer would be welcome in any lodge from here to the camps of the *Quahadi*," Toby insisted when he and Jim talked this over between them, on the far side of the fire from Prince Frederick William's learned men of science. "He would be an honored man, no matter where he went and never lack for a meal."

"Or a patient," Jim agreed. "But he is supposed to be the scientific advisor to his Prince, not a wandering medical missionary, and we're supposed to be keeping them from wandering off or getting killed. And the longer we're …"

That was when the young Comanche appeared at their fire, and spoke a few words to Toby, who rose from where he had been squatting on the ground. "His uncle wishes to speak with us now," Toby reported. "He says that Red Knife can see … not well, but better than in many moons."

"That's more than I was expecting," Jim hardly dared to breath, as Tony gestured Doctor Maier to join them. Nerves wound as tight as fiddle-strings, he walked at Doctor Maier's side, only slightly relieved at this good report. Now, if he could only convince the good doctor to move east, out of Comanche lands…

In obedience to Doctor Maier's orders, Red Knife was lying flat on his back in the shadow of a crude brush arbor. His head was still braced by the sacks of sand, and the silent girl knelt at his feet, a small lather parfleche bag at her side. When Toby, Doctor Maier and Jim came within his limited sight, he raised one hand slightly and began to speak. Again, Toby relayed his words.

"He says that he can see again, now. Not as he could when he was young – but he can, and he will soon regain his strength and vigor. He wishes to reward you with the greatest gift which he can command at this time."

"There is no need for that," Doctor Maier made a polite objection, but Toby continued.

"He wishes to gift you with a woman. His nephews say you have none of your own."

"I…" Completely flummoxed, Doctor Maier could only gape like a fish, as Toby continued.

"They call her Nauta and she will serve you well. She is only the least of his slaves, and his youngest wife is jealous of her anyway."

"I…" Doctor Maier stuttered. "I do not …."

"Yes, you do," Jim spoke through thinned lips. "It would be a dangerous discourtesy to spurn the gift of a great warrior like Red Knife. Put a smile on your face, Doctor, and thank him for his generosity."

"But a … a slave! And a woman!" Doctor Maier blinked in pure bewilderment. Toby and Jim exchanged a look.

"Smile and nod," Jim ordered, his own countenance carefully bland. "Thank Red Knife and his nephews, Brother." He hissed an aside to Toby, as the girl stood, her buffalo-skin bag in her hands. "We'll sort out what to do with the girl … Miss Nauta – later."

"I don't know what to do with a woman!" Doctor Maier protested, as they walked away, and Toby snorted on a stifled laugh. The girl Nauta followed them at several paces, her eyes downcast.

"Not my problem, Doctor," Jim said, out of the corner of his mouth as they returned to their own campsite. Doctor Maier sank into one of the folding camp chairs, wiping his glasses on an immaculate white handkerchief, while Nauta sat at his feet with her bag, looking expectantly at him.

"They gave me a woman!" Doctor Maier was still utterly rattled. "I don't know what to do with this madness, Graff, I truly don't! What will His Highness say to this?" Von Brockdorff set down his pipe and commented mildly, "Interesting schedule of fees in this place, Herr Doctor. I take it you could not gracefully refuse?"

"Frankly, I think the Widow Jackson will be more than pleased to solve this puzzle for you." Jim interposed. "I would just give Miss Nauta over to her care and we'll sort out the long-term questions as soon as we are away from this place. And he could not refuse. The Comanche may be unlettered savages, but they know the difference between courtesy and insult. And if you think they don't, then insult them and see what happens. Just ensure that Mr. Shaw and I have a fair start on good horses when you do."

Doctor Maier dropped his head into his hands, moaning. "This is *unglaublich* – unthinkable! A slave! What is to be done!?"

Jim felt a certain amount of pity for the doctor's distress. Yes, there were some matters which his medical education and service to a German prince clearly had not prepared him. He raised his voice. "Mrs. Jackson ... where are you? We have a task, a new task which requires your motherly touch." He feared for a moment that the good widow had somehow been whisked away, but she appeared from beyond the nearest wagon, somewhat pink in the face and out of breath.

"I am here, Mr. Reade – whatever is the ... oh, my stars and garters! What is that poor Meskin child doing here!"

"It appears that she has been gifted to us, in thanks for deliverance from blindness," That was Mr. Achtenberg, bland and omni-competent, his arms full of supplies from the wagon, appearing like a species of Germanic genii on the Widow Jackson's heels.

As Jim expected, the widow straightened her redoubtable shoulders, as he explained, "Red Knife has given her to Doctor Maier out of gratitude. We will put her in your care, ma'am, until we can return her to her family in Mexico."

"You may depend on me!" The Widow Jackson exclaimed. "That poor child – tell her, Mr. Shaw! We'll see that she is safe and returned, all proper! She has nothing to fear from any of the gennelmen, no, I will see to that! She will be as safe as a baby in her mother's arms, we'll see to that, for certain!"

The girl looked from the Widow Jackson, as wary as a small trapped wild animal, as Toby relayed all that in the guttural Comanche tongue, and then nodded submissively and answered in a few barely-whispered words.

"She says that she will obey her new master and mistress. She is a good girl and has always obeyed. She says that her name when she was a child was Mina. But she cannot remember anything else, since she has been with the Comanche since then."

"We'll see what we can do for the poor child!" The Widow's expression was one of iron-clad determination; Jim didn't doubt that she would do exactly that. What he had not expected was how thoroughly Widow Jackson would take over the care of Nauta-once-Mina, of some small unknown settlement in the North of Mexico, as the exploratory journey of the three learned men continued through the rest of Texas.

***

They packed up and moved the wagon and their train of horses and pack animals the very next morning, Mina sitting straight and upright on the wagon seat next to the Widow Jackson. She did not look back at the Comanche camp, only straight ahead.

"Poor little thing," the Widow Jackson exclaimed. "She has no notion of what to expect – and I dessay that she doesn't remember much. How old do you think she was when she was captured by them red heathens … begging your pardon, Mr. Shaw, I am sure."

Toby shook his head; he strode along next to the slowly-turning wagon wheel, with his long tomahawk resting on his shoulder. "Older than an infant. She says that the top of her head came to the belly of a horse when they came to her village – so, say three or four summers. Old enough to not be a trouble, old enough to be set to work."

"I have tried a bit of that Spanish lingo on her," the Widow Jackson continued. "For I speak a bit of it, enough to do business with them as don't have any proper English in them. But she doesn't seem to understand."

"Not surprising," Toby replied, courteously omitting a mention that the Widow Jackson likely spoke Spanish very badly to start with. "Taken so young, she would have forgotten, through never speaking it again."

"Then I shall have to teach her proper English," the widow announced, "And mebbe Mr. Achterberg or the other gentlemen could teach her that German lingo. She looks like a clever enough girl, I reckon she could learn it quick enough."

Jim, riding along the other side of the wagon and overhearing this conversation, thought that the good widow was vastly overstating her own ability as a mentor ... until a week had passed by his estimation, and Mina followed the Widow Jackson's direction when it came to fixing meals over the open fire and Mr. Achterberg's commands in German as well. After several more weeks of their wandering journey had passed, and they had paused briefly in half-deserted Austin on the Colorado, and in Bastrop – Mina wore a proper calico dress and a white apron when she assisted the Widow Jackson in serving the meals. Jim had no notion of where, or how the Widow Jackson had contrived dress, apron, and starched white cap, or even convinced the girl to wear them, even if she was still shod in buffalo-hide moccasins. This was a woman-mystery, one that he did not wish to have any intimate acquaintance with; a thing best managed by women.

At the end of summer, they returned to Galveston, where a tall-masted ship under the command of a German master and commander awaited Prince Frederick Williams' wandering men of science. The end of his and Toby's assignment was in sight, physically and metaphorically. There was hardly any more opportunity for the missions of those men of science to go embarrassingly astray, or so Jim assumed, right up until the night of their last encampment near Goose Greek, at the mouth of Trinity Bay. In the morning, the Widow Jackson, Corb, and Mina would start west with the wagon, home to Copano, while the remainder of the party – Doctor Maier, Professor Kraus and the Graff, with their entourage and vast collection of specimens, maps and sketches – would take passage on a river steamboat to Galveston, and from there to their homes in Germany. It had been a surprisingly enjoyable summer, after the rocky start, what with Professor Kraus' duel, Doctor Maier's medical practice among the wild Comanche, and the Widow Jackson's matrimonial designs against von Brockdorff.

"I think we are nearly home free," Jim remarked, as dusk settled over their camp. Fireflies twinkled in the tall stands of grass at the water's edge, and the first evening stars were showing themselves in the darkening sky. "The Prince should be happy with what his men of science have found. That will make President Jones happy, because the Prince's investment in Texas will come through. Jack will be happy, because there will be money in the government's treasury. We will be happy because we may get paid."

The cook-fire burned bright in the twilight, and the inside of the tents glowed as if they were paper lanterns. The sounds of raised voices in German came from the largest of them, and Toby shrugged. "It doesn't sound as if von Brockdorff is very happy ..."

"Nor Mrs. Jackson," Jim noted. Some five minutes previously, the Widow Jackson and Mr. Achterberg had gone into the big tent and closed the tent-flap openings behind them. "I expect that she has now to make clear what she wants and more than just payment for the hire of herself and her wagon for the summer." Her voice was discretely low, as was Mr. Achterberg's, but the Graff von Brockdorff had no such reserve, and his anger was obvious, even if his words were not.

At that moment, young Corb Jackson approached the simple canvas shelter where Jim and Toby were accustomed to shelter in at night – open to the air, their bedrolls set on armfuls of cut fresh branches or rush. Corb, fourteen and rather awkward with it, was a quietly competent youth. All the summer long he had been as obedient to his formidable mother as he had been admiring of Jim and Toby. Fortunately, his hero-worship had not been so obvious as to be embarrassing. Jim liked the boy; he was man enough to follow orders, yet think on his feet, so he had Corb marked down as a possible 'stiletto-man' recruit, once he had a bit more seasoning on him and at least one enlistment in a Ranger company under his belt.

"We'll be packin' up and heading home first thing," he said. "Soon as we break camp." He sank onto the horse-blanket that formed the visiting area of Jim and Toby's portion of camp. "Ma says she wants to see how the garden has done … and how Matt and Sarah did with the place. She's right pleased over employment with the Dutch gentlemen," Corb added hastily, and Jim grinned.

"Well, since she has got a husband out of it," he said. Corb also grinned. "He's a daisy, ain't he? Ma is well pleased. Says there ain't nothing like having a man about the place. Mr. Jackson was only my step-pa, but he did all right with us. They say that Ma is a right good judge of a man."

"She is that," Jim touched a dry twig to the fire, and lit his evening tobacco pipe with it. "Your mother is the finest cook that I know, far better than my own mother. Once the *Mary Clifton* delivers us to Galveston in two days, I will have to endure some days of Mama baking treats and turnovers for us…"

"I like your mother's turnovers," Toby interjected, and Jim laughed. "You have low tastes, Brother. Fortunate that my mother thinks the world of you, and among your people, mothers rule the roost. So, young Corb; do you think that you will like your sainted mother as a baroness, the ruler of a drafty castle demesne in Prussia?"

"I don't know what you mean, Captain Reade?" Corb Jackson looked honestly baffled. "It's Mr. Emil – that is, Mr. Achterberg that Ma is marrying. As soon as she can get him to a preacher, or an alcalde. He's going to come with us to Copano, y'see. I like him fine enough. He an' Ma are just now telling Mr. Brockdorff of their intent and collecting our wages for the summer's work."

"She ... she's intent on marrying Mr. Achterberg?" Jim felt as if he had been smacked in the bread-basket. Mr. Achterberg, bland and mild, the rock of service upon which his lord and master depended? No wonder that the Graff was angry. To his great annoyance, Toby was grinning over his own astonishment. "I thought certain that it was the Graff she had her cap set for; a title and a castle and god knows that all."

Even Corb was grinning now. "Him? Ma says he's nothing but a puffed-up turkey-cock. But he paid her an' me durned well for a couple of months work. Mebbe we can put on another room to the house, now. Ma says that Mr. Emil is just to her taste, an' a nice gentleman and all. Too good to be at the beck and call of the likes of Mr. Brockdorff, and deserving of his own establishment."

"Better to be at the beck and call of your Ma," Jim allowed. But there was still a consideration; how angered would the Graff be? Angry enough to advise the Prince against the investment of his consortium of nobles in Texas? He said as much to Corb, who shrugged and replied,

"Ma says that he isn't the sort to hold a grudge like that. He's hasty-tempered and all, but he is a gentleman of science."

"I guess that we'll have to wait and see," Jim sighed, as a portion of his burden or worry fell back onto his shoulders, just as the flap of von Brockdorff's tent was thrown back. The Widow Jackson and Mr. Achterberg emerged; both looking quite pleased.

"Well, Corb," Mrs. Jackson patted her son's shoulder and exclaimed, "We are away in the morning, you and I, and Emil and that poor Mina child. Himself even gave an extry purse just for her – a dower, he said it was, for when she was grown and wished to marry. Rough as a cob he may be, but he's a fair man and no mistake, and sorry I am for having misjudged him on the basis of his manner."

Mr. Achterberg nodded in solemn agreement. "A very forward-thinking and truthful gentleman, that is certain. But lacking a certain gift of diplomacy."

"That's what I'm afraid of," Jim sighed.

***

He should not have worried – the three gentlemen of science, with Haun and Fuchs in attendance over their mound of luggage set sail without further incident, while white seabirds soared over the masts of the tall ship which was to carry them all back to Bremen. Professor Kraus and Doctor Maier both wrung Jim and Toby's hand, proclaiming their gratitude, and pledging friendship.

"Your splendid geography!" enthused Professor Kraus. "Be assured of my favorable report to His Highness!"

"I myself may yet return, once I have made my formal report," Doctor Maier wiped some moisture from thick glasses with the end of the scarf around his neck. "Regardless of His Highness's eventual determination. There is a crying need for a trained practitioner of the medical arts … and the weather is so very temperate, compared to that of Prussia in the winter...*auf weiderseihen*, Captain Reade, Mr. Shaw, until we meet again!"

Even von Brockdorff sounded completely in earnest. He crushed the bones of Jim's hand and then to Jim's astonishment, snapped a military salute. "Captain Reade! You have been of inestimable value to our party. You have my thanks for your efforts on our behalf. I cannot presume to say what His Highness will eventually decide regarding this Texas adventure, but rest assured that my report will contain nothing but favorable comment on the efforts of yourself, and your government."

"Thank you, Graff," Jim returned the salute, feeling like an almighty fool about it. Feeling even more like a fool when Fuchs and Haun did the same, both promising to remember their adventures and associations in Texas, as well as an eventual return under the auspices of Prince Frederick William's consortium.

"Oh, yah, the noble gentlemen are all for this," Haun pumped Jim's hand as if he expected to get water from a deep well of it. "And I shall ask for a place in their venture. For they will need soldiers, yah?" He dropped a broad wink, and lowered his voice to an envious-sounding chuckle. "Those women of Texas – they need good husbands, too? Achterberg, he did well; a woman who owns a boarding house and a grog-shop? Paradise! *Sehr gut!*"

"We will be happy to see your return," Jim murmured. Fuchs briefly shook his hand and followed his comrade up the gangway to the ship, which now – to the tune of much shouting from a man on the deck with a speaking-tube – was letting out her white sails from the many masts. They billowed like clouds, filling with the wind, as the ship's crew cast-off and drew away, out into the waters of the harbor – and then out into the open blue waters of the Gulf.

"Think they were saying true, Brother?" Jim asked, as he and Toby turned away from the last sight of the German ship vanishing

136

into the distance around. It was bad luck to watch a ship out of sight. That's what Emily Reade had always said, and she was from a seafaring Massachusetts family and who would better know?

"I have no way of judging the words of the gentlemen of your science," Toby grinned. "But they sounded with truth in them to me. I am hungry, Brother – let us go to your mother's house, and see if she has a meal prepared for us."

5 – Into the Wilds
The Fifth Adventure

Wherein Jim and Toby join with a US Army expedition to the unexplored southwest – am expedition with a secret mission!

"I came as soon as I received your message," Toby Shaw arrived at the Bullock House in Austin where Jack Hays and Jim Reade had taken rooms while they awaited the arrival of Jim's trusted fellow 'stiletto-man' on before the meeting with Governor Wood. The stage from Fort Belknap delivered Toby promptly on the third day after their arrival; Toby resplendent in a well-cut suit, fashionable cravat, waistcoat and white shirt – his long braids the only jarring note in his otherwise conventional appearance. "What is so important regarding this task that we are both bidden to Austin?"

"I have no idea," Jim answered. "Colonel Hays has been remarkably close-mouthed on that score … as always."

"Part of my ingratiating personal charm," Jack replied, with a hearty handshake. "Sit down, sit down … and I have no notion of the purpose myself. I know – difficult to credit. But I've been away for months, and had a war with Mexico to win, so I've lost touch with the day to day of things. I've organized a private supper, so that we can catch up – and not set gossiping tongues to wagging. Since it is the Governor himself driving this … I can only speculate that it is something to do with the United States."

"Of which we are now one, since Annexation," Jim pointed out. "And with the US Army to see to our security – what purpose do we have now? Toby and I, and your handful of other stiletto fellows?"

"Oh, there are purposes," Jack replied. "One or two, still left to us as Rangers. I believe that the Governor will be prompt in relieving all our curiosity tomorrow morning. We are bidden to a private conference at nine of the clock at the capitol building, and not to breath a word to anyone of this. It appears to be an extremely sensitive matter."

"Aren't all of them?" Jim raised an eyebrow. Jack laughed, and then his expression turned melancholy.

"Most of them, I think. I fear that the feats performed by my stiletto-men Rangers will never be made public; only recorded in certain dusty archives and locked in a sturdy iron safe for all eternity."

"Well, we didn't get into it for the glory, did we, Toby?" Jim shrugged philosophically. "We did it for ... because it was in the cause of justice." His blood-brother laughed, replying, "Justice, in the way of your courts, James-Reade-Esquire? We perform our tasks because it is right to do. If the Great Spirit alone knows – why then, what does it matter to us?"

"Well-said, boys," Jack regarded the two with approval, and Jim thought that he looked ... well, wearier and older. The brief sharp war with Mexico had aged their commander. A fair number of his old Ranger comrades had fallen in that field; Addison Gillespie and Sam Walker dead on campaign, and one of his oldest Ranger associates sidelined by wounds and walking away when his final enlistment was done. But it was as if Jack intuited that thought of Jim's – for he smiled immediately, and exclaimed,

"I know the cooking at Bullock's isn't a patch on the market ladies in Bexar with their pots of good red stew – but I have an appetite tonight! Shall we swap stretchers about what we all have been up to since the last time we met?"

"I thought you would never ask," Jim answered – and so the evening passed agreeably enough, especially since Jack produced a bottle of good bourbon whiskey – "From Kentucky, a gift from a good friend!" Jack insisted, although Jim had suspicions, since the bottle was absent any label. And Toby foreswore any of it, unless well-diluted with water, saying only that although he was not of the temperance persuasion, and not adverse entirely toward a jolly evening with old friends, he did not care to partake of liquor at full-strength.

***

In the morning, Jack, Toby, and Jim strolled the short way up Congress Street to the frame capitol building which edifice crowned the top of the hill – a commanding height in Austin, which had been built in a fair and parklike meadow, dotted by copses of noble oak and cypress trees, and threaded through with creeks of clear water. Now the heights to north and south of the great silver sweep of the Colorado River looked down upon a city invigorated by the peace which followed on the successful prosecution of a war, and the consummation of a marriage between an independent Texas and the United States; a marriage which canny old General Sam Houston had labored to arrange for ten long and bitter years. Still, Jim slightly regretted the surrender of a state of independency. It meant that the Rangers were no longer needed; now the US Army, dressed in their fine blue coats and commanded by gold-braid-hung officers would be responsible for the frontier ... and for those matters of security which had been Jack's particular responsibility. Perhaps his term as one of Jack's stiletto-men was also at an end, a matter about which he was in two minds. His father was old, yet still vigorous in the practice of law, and their joint practice in Galveston gave every sign of being lively and prosperous, could Jim only pay considerable more of his time and energies to it.

If Toby felt something of the same regrets, he gave no sign of it, as they crossed the porch of that white-washed frame building which served as the capital, and stood in the entryway. The door stood halfway open to a hallway. They were a few minutes early, by Jim's stout hunter watch.

Without hesitation, Jack thumped on the door panel with his fists, and called, "Say, anyone at home? I'm Colonel Hays, and we have an appointment with Governor Wood."

"At least I didn't have my heart seat on a grand reception," Jim remarked, and Toby – standing at several paces behind, peered over Jack's shoulder, saying, "Maybe we should ask that soldier?"

Hearing those words, a stocky, grizzled man in US Army blue sprang from a seat at the foot of the stairs, straightening in attention and rendering a crisp salute. His sleeves bore a great number of stripes, testifying to the solid character of the man and his value to the federal Army. "Colonel Hays, sah! I was told to expect you at any moment. The gentlemen are waiting upstairs. If you and your good gentlemen would be so kind as to follow after me. The General is a man who esteems punctuality."

"Thank you, Sergeant," Jack returned the salute with a nod, never having been much of one for military protocol and the practice thereof. "Have you any notion of what this is about, Sergeant …"

"Owen, sah – and I do, but I have been given the strictest of orders, straight from the General, which the Senator hisself approved in the next breath."

"I expect that it is a matter of national importance then?" Jim ventured, as they climbed the stairs, and Sergeant Owen looked over his shoulder at them. Jim wondered why the man seemed so familiar, in a way that suggested a previous encounter had not been a pleasant one.

"In a manner o' speaking. But if you ken the matter properly – there is a touch o' the personal as well. And to more than just to the Senator. But," Sergeant Owen recovered his sense of discretion, a sense which warred against the habit of NCOs to pass along interesting gossip and speculations. "I should say no more, properly. But it is personal to me as well. Captain O'Neill was … well, he was one of the good ones." Ah – English; Jim made a note to himself, and a reminder to conceal at all costs his instinctive dislike of the man. Owen was very like that English agent who had been involved in the matter of the old Casa Wilkinson … and more balefully, in the lost San Saba Treasure.

"Captain O'Neill?" Toby looked across at Jim, as they followed Jack and Sergeant Owen up the stairs at a discreet distance. "What of this – and what to do with us, James Reade Esquire?"

"I can't be certain," Jim whispered back. "But if he means Captain Brendan O'Neill – and I am thinking that he must – the Captain was one of the rising bright stars in the Army, if the newspapers have it right. A favored child of fortune, as my father would put it. A graduate of West Point, although his background was hardly favorable, being the child of poor Irish immigrants. He was taken prisoner in the fighting around Monterray and treated brutally, but made a daring escape to our lines on the city outskirts. Fought in the thickest and bloodiest part of it – wounded a couple of times, until he was finally sent home. Feted all around Washington and promoted for his trouble. Then he was given command of an expedition into the western territories, even before they were turned over as part of the peace settlement."

"Ah then," Toby whispered, as Sergeant Owen approached a door at the head of the stairs. "He was favored by the great chiefs to lead a war party."

"Not a war party," Jim corrected him. "A party of exploration; to make maps of land features, find natural roads, and make friends with the Indian tribes, in the expectation of making allies among them."

"A far-thinking notion," Toby nodded. "Most uncharacteristic of what I have seen so far of the Yengies. What has this matter to do with us?"

"Likely because he never came back from it," was all that Jim could say before Sergeant Owen rapped briefly on the closed door at the top of the stairs. At a word from inside, Sergeant Owen opened the door and announced in a stentorian voice reminiscent of a parade ground, "Colonel Hays, with…"

"Captain Reade and Mr. Shaw," Jack stepped through the door, while Jim winced. Yes, a captaincy was a nice thing to have, but it was more for a show of authority – a courtesy title, rather than working rank. On the other hand, he reflected as he followed Jack and regarded the four men within, it was a small but significant thing, in their eyes.

The room was an office of sorts; a fairly workmanlike one, with several crude desks, lined with shelves of books and boxes of documents along the inner walls, and a small table and several chairs by the window. There were four men in the office, one of whom Jim knew instantly to be important, because he was Jack's higher commander; Governor Wood. Of the other three, two were in uniform – again, the blue of the federal Army, but only the older of the pair was anyone to command respect. The younger lingered by the doorway with Sgt. Owen, for the older officer and the gent in the expensive waistcoat had commanded the scattering of chairs by the window.

"Colonel Hays," the older officer rose and extended his hand – a fit-appearing gentleman in middle years, his hair and impressive mustache and side-whiskers only lightly touched with gray. "My pleasure – Joe Barnes. We met briefly after Saltillo, although you had so much on your plate at that time, with the press of war to prosecute and your Rangers to command, that I will not hold it against you should you not recollect that previous occasion."

"But I do recall you – and with appreciation," Jack returned the courtesy. "You did us good service, my Rangers and I, after Saltillo. You were a god-send for my fellows… forgive me, I recall what men were able to do for my people, but not the rank or the office they held when doing it."

"Supply Corps," General Barnes returned, with good humor. "A necessary, yet underrated department. A matter of ledgers, lists, and registers, of figures and supplies, but the great Napoleon himself observed that an Army marches on its stomach."

"And is this a matter of concern to the Supply Corps?" Jack went to the point of this meeting without any fanfare, and Governor Wood sighed.

"Brass tacks," he observed with a glance ceilingward. "That's what I have always liked about you, Jack – not wasting any time getting down to them."

"The matter upon which you and your agents have been summoned is actually a matter of national pride; only peripherally a matter most personal to me," answered the gentleman in the expensively ornate waistcoat. "Randall Bartlett, of Kentucky, Colonel Hays. I do have an interest regarding the whereabouts – or even the survival of Captain O'Neill." The gentleman's florid countenance turned briefly mournful. "Before his disappearance, he was – he is engaged to my daughter, Rebecca. Gentlemen, if you have no daughters, you have no idea of the wiles which they can wind around your heart. My darling Rebecca has been waging a campaign of the kind which no mortal father can stand long against – find her beloved, she implores me; find him and restore him to her, or her heart will break. 'Papa' she begged me, 'you have influential friends, important friends, you can surely exchange favors.'" Senator Bartlett offered a small and very wry smile. "I do not ordinarily trade on my office for personal consideration, gentlemen – but I must admit that if Captain O'Neill's aged mother, a sister or an affianced other than my Rebecca had come and begged me to do what I could … I fear that I would be making the same request of you that I am making now. Find Captain O'Neill. General Barnes is among my oldest friends; and able to facilitate this meeting and sponsor my request of you."

"Understood," Jack Hays nodded. "But I still wonder, gentlemen – since he wasn't our concern when he was – er, misplaced somewhere in the new western territories, why should you come to us, ask my fellows for their assistance? I might have thought this was the business of the US Army."

"So it would have been," General Barnes replied warmly. "But there is a potential complication, one which might prove embarrassing. And that is why outsiders such as your compatriots are involved. The matter is of the utmost delicacy." He cast a significant look at Governor Wood.

"Jack – I'll be in my own office," Governor Wood nodded. "If you wish to speak with me when the gentlemen are finished briefing you on this particular … engagement." The Governor absented himself from the dusty office with efficient dispatch, although Jim wondered if this was such a matter of delicacy, why Sergeant Owen and the unnamed young officer remained, hovering at the door as if they were hounds bidden to stay, yet uncertain of their welcome within the circle. Jack claimed the last chair, and eyed General Barnes and Senator Bartlett as they resumed their seats.

"How exactly did you come to lose track of your heroic young captain? You may speak freely, as Captain Reade and Mr. Shaw will be the Texas men of my department dispatched on this errand. And what is the exact nature of this delicate matter?"

"Sergeant Owen is the one most able to answer that question," General Barnes replied, "As part of Captain O'Neill's exploration party, and the senior NCO remaining. Sergeant, would you explain the situation?"

"Gladly, sah!" Sergeant Owen stepped forward, assuming an attitude of formal parade-rest before the half-circle of chairs, and fixing his eyes on the farther wall – a thing which Jim found vaguely irritating. It was as if the man were performing in a pantomime. "We set out early in the spring of last year from Shreveport, our mission being to follow the old trail to Santa Fe, and then to strike northwesterly from there, to map the uncharted wastelands, and search out a certain river – a river of significant size, which was reported by Spanish explorers many years ago. It was the conviction of Captain O'Neill that this river, if navigable by craft of any size, might provide a most expeditious route to California… The great Colorado, they call it. Means "Red" so I am told."

"Did you locate this river, then?" Jack cut into the flow of words. "And at what point was Captain O'Neill lost to your part?"

"Indeed we did, sah!" Sergeant Owen answered warmly. "And the part of it which we explored – so sublime a sight as may hardly be imagined! Grooved deep into the earth, attended by mighty rock towers and cliffs striped in red, orange, gold – the colors of flame, in the sunlight of a dying day. I have seen many splendors on this earth, gentleman, but that grand river, cradled in its mighty red canyon …" he shook his head. "Captain O'Neill waxed even more poetic. He was like a boy in a toy-shop, sah, marveling at everything. Nothing would content him than to essay a venture down to the water-edge with a corporal and two private soldiers of our party, leaving me in charge of the remainder. They carried a patent collapsible boat with them, intending to venture a little way down the river. We were to be collecting geological and botanical specimens, y'see, while we waited on Captain O'Neill's return in a fortnight."

"That was perilous, to so split your party in that fashion," Jack remarked, with veiled disapproval. "Especially when you are uncertain of the friendliness of the local Indian folk."

"Not so," Sergeant Owen demurred. "The natives were of a nature inclined to be friendly; farming folk in the main. They make baskets and pottery, grow crops of maize and orchard fruit as fine as any Christian. Although they would make bonny warriors if rightly provoked, they do not live for it, as do the Comanche, and export war wholesale."

"Well, that's some comfort," General Barnes remarked, in some relief. "Hear that, young Joe? No chances of death or glory against the wild Comanche for you this journey! Just bring back your old playfellows' dearest, and that should be sufficient reward."

"I heard, sir," the young officer answered, with easy familiarity. "I suppose Becky will weep all over me in that case – and I will be forgiven for teasing her so mercilessly when we were children."

"It depends," General Barnes smiled. "Colonel Hays; my son, Lieutenant Barnes. He is newly-graduated, and will be a part of your expedition at his insistence. Captain O'Neill was an upper-classman, and much revered among the junior cadets. His orders, and those for Sergeant Owen are all cut and approved. I hope that you will forgive my presumption," he added, looking searchingly at Jack, Jim and Toby. "But for reasons of security, I prefer to involve only family and those connections of proven discretion, in addition to your people, Colonel Hays. There is one other, who will be a part of this expedition, although he is not privy to the entire story … continue, Sergeant."

"Thank you, sah!" Sergeant Owen fixed his gaze on the opposite wall. Jim was quite certain this was not for any intrinsic beauty of the wall itself, as it was an uninspiring collection of rough shelves, and a tattered map of Texas tacked to that part not covered with shelves and stacked with ledgers. Jim murmured an aside to his blood-brother, "So we are getting to the part about how they misplaced their hero and how that came to be a potential embarrassment to the federal Army."

"We waited for seventeen days," Sergeant Owen continued, still staring at the wall. "I was disinclined, sah, to split our party even further, in sending out a small detachment to search for Captain O'Neill. He was a man of his word; if he said he would return in a fortnight, then he would return in a fortnight. If he did not, he said that I should use my best judgment in that eventuality. The Captain reposed a great deal of trust in me," Sergeant Owen added with a touch of modest pride. "Since I have soldiered, man and boy for more than thirty years and under three flags, counting this one."

"Likely you have forgotten more of the trade than many have ever learned," General Barnes agreed. "As a Living Rule of the art of soldiering. I cannot say that such trust was misplaced."

"Thank you, sah," Sergeant Owen unbent sufficiently to look directly at his small audience, and Jack cleared his throat. "And on the seventeenth day," he asked, quietly.

Sergeant Owen's gaze snapped back to the wall. "On the seventeenth day, Corporal Mayhew staggered into our camp in a most piteous condition. The corporal was one of the party accompanying the Captain. He was nearly dead from exposure, hunger, and thirst, besides having half his ribs stove in. But he was able to tell us of what happened; on the eighth day of their explorations of the river, the boat was taken by a sudden swift current, swept over a waterfall, and smashed on the rocks below. Private MacLean and Private Josephson were killed in falling or drowned in deep water. Captain O'Neill's leg was broken, most painfully, and he had an almighty crack to the skull. He could not walk, and was unconscious for some time. Mayhew was hurt only a little less severely, but he managed to pull Captain O'Neill to safety, in a little cove sheltered by a cliff overhang. He left the Captain comfortably settled in that shelter, with a water-bottle, and what he could retrieve of the supplies. He gathered wood, built a small fire, administered what doctoring he could render and went to fetch aid from our main camp. He was four or five days at that … venturing back along the riverbank, and climbing back up along the path they had followed going down. He was …" Sergeant Owen's harsh voice roughened. "In no very good condition, sah. He was crawling on hands and knees at the last, and only lived a day or so – just long enough to tell us of what had happened."

"A brave young man," Senator Bartlett remarked, much moved, although he must have heard the story at least once before. "And a credit to the uniform, and to his commander."

"No, sah, in a spirit of honesty, I would beg to disagree," Sergeant Owen continued his rigid examination of the wall. "He was addicted to strong drink and consorting w' women of the disreputable class. I did not think he was of the stuff that the best are made of – but he did well enough, for all o' that, and died doing his duty."

"Nothing in his life became him so much as his manner of leaving it, eh?" Senator Bartlett commented, and Sergeant Owen appeared even grimmer than before.

"Aye so. Well, he was thorough enough – poor lad – when it came to marking his trail. We followed it easily, but upon finding the cove and cave where Captain O'Neill had been, there was nothing save the ashes of a dead fire and a few scraps of the rubberized canvas from the remains of the boat. That was how we were certain of the place, sah; the bits of the boat, y'see. The Captain was gone. "We searched the nearby riverbanks as carefully as we could on foot, having lost use of the boat." Sergeant Owen's eyes returned to the tattered map on the wall opposite. "And found no other trace of the Captain, although we found and buried Private Josephson alongside Corporal Mayhew. Having done so, we made all speed to return east and file reports, along with the maps and samples, and considered the expedition completed."

"Ah, then – that is how they lost him," Jim murmured to his blood-brother, as they watched this with interest. "In a delirium, fallen into the river, and carried away. No doubt of it."

"But I do not understand the requirement for secrecy," Jack cleared his throat. "Sad enough to lose a man in that manner – injured and alone in the wilderness, and of course his loved ones would grieve his loss, but I simply do not see this as a matter of ..."

"There's more to this," General Barnes held up a hand. "Thank you, Sergeant – I'll carry on from here. You will see the need for discretion when I am finished. The following spring, there was a small story in the weekly *St. Louis Register* which excited much comment; a tale by a pair of Mormon missionaries searching for converts among the heathen – a tale of a white man living among a tribe settled along the river … which from our calculations was not far from where Captain O'Neill and his party came to grief. It struck me as a curious coincidence and I made further inquiries. The original story was printed in the *California Star* – the proprietor is a Mormon, you see, and would know of such incidents involving his coreligionists. Two weeks ago, a messenger returned from California with urgent dispatches – and a fuller accounting of the missionaries visit to the Havasuopii village, including a physical description of the white man. He was tall, with sandy-colored hair, and walked with a bad limp."

"There must be any number of white renegades and mountain men, even captives taken as children," Jack pointed out. Jim nodded; he knew of at least a dozen such, captured as children raised as Indians, and adopted into their tribe. "What of your missing Private McLean? He was reported drowned as well – but perhaps…"

"McLean was a dark Scot, near as dark as an Indian himself," Sergeant Owen interjected. "And no' what you would call tall. But I take your point, Colonel, sah, regarding renegades and such. But the description of this man also made note of a peculiar scar on his cheek. The Captain had such a scar, gotten in the fighting at Monterrey."

"You see, Colonel," General Barnes sighed heavily. "It very well might be O'Neill. And if it is – it means that an officer of this Army has deserted his duties, his loved ones – his very life among civilized people. The embarrassment to the Army, to our government, after having proclaimed him a hero, honored and decorated will be enormous, if word got out. It may be also that he was deprived of his memory through that blow to the head, in which case he must be returned to us, that he might be restored to family and career. In either case, we simply must resolve this matter and mystery, and do so without causing an embarrassing scandal. I know that you and your people can be trusted to be discrete; such discretion is not only the better part of valor, it is also the better part of diplomacy. Only those of us within this room know the full import of this mission."

There was silence in the musty office for a long moment, while motes of dust danced in the slanted sunlight coming through the glazed window.

Finally, Jack spoke. "You fellows have taken in all that? Good." He fixed General Barnes and the Senator with his sternest gaze. "Jim Reade and Toby Shaw are two of the best I have – you just say the word, and when you want them to leave."

"Excellent, Colonel!" General Barnes beamed. "Then in two weeks, from Camp Verde – where the fifth of this venture will join you. Ned Beale – he's a Navy man, but knows the west about as well as any of us landlubbers. There will be your lads, my son and Sergeant Owen – only you four know the real purpose of this mission!"

"Pardon me for inquiring," Jim spoke in his normal voice for almost the first time in this interview. "But – why Camp Verde? We can just as well depart from here. I have my own trash and traps, Mr. Shaw has his; we are in expectation of heading off into whichever direction Colonel Jack sends us on a moment's notice."

"Because that is where you will collect up the camels!" General Barnes replied, with a mighty laugh at the expression which had descended on all their faces – Sergeant Owen's excepted. Jim could only think that he had become well-accustomed to insane requirements while in service to his variable flags.

∗∗∗

"Camels!" Ned Beale exclaimed in delight, when he showed Jim and Toby their means of transport at least as far as the fabled canyon of the Colorado in the vast New Mexico Territory. Beale was a little younger than Jim, a lively and gangly young Yankee with a high sloping forehead which merged into a magnificently beaky nose adorned at the lower margin with an equally magnificent and bushy mustache. His Navy rank on a strength report was a relatively lowly one – but his functioning level appeared to be much higher, due to friends in high places and to his recent daring exploits in crossing the continent several times on his own, armored with nothing but a spirit of his own recklessness. With a certain sinking of heart, Jim realized that here was another enthusiast with an insatiable appetite for adventure, for experiences and arcane knowledge. Not that there was anything amiss with such qualities, in moderation – but individuals possessing an excess of them were apt to go haring off in unexpected and usually dangerous tangents. "Ain't they a marvel? And what better use for traversing the vast deserts than creatures ideally suited to it! They carry burdens which would buckle the knees of half a dozen mules, without complaint, go for days without food and water …"

"They look like a horse designed by a government committee, smell like Satan's own privy, and frighten the daylights out of all the horses, mules and oxen around," Jim replied, refusing to be moved by Ned's enthusiasm.

"But you see, Jim – I may call you Jim, may I? And you should call me Ned, of course. They are perfectly designed by nature for the harsh climes of this new territory! What better use can we make of them… I am charged to explore the natural route to California from Texas and to see how the camels perform …Hey, Walid Ali – what do you think of their fitness for six months in crossing the southern deserts?"

"A desert – like any other, sire," replied one of the beasts' hired handlers, a wiry sun-burned man, who wouldn't have appeared out of place in a Ranger company, save that his head was wrapped in a turban of fine green cloth. He spoke English fluently enough, although with a strange accent. The other handler looked off into the distance; he was an older man with a thick gray-streaked beard, who never spoke, but was usually to be found somewhere about the camel corral.

"Nonetheless, I am not riding on one of those critters," Jim announced, flatly. "I'll stick to the evil I know, rather than fly to that which I know nothing of."

"You have no sense of adventure, Jim," Ned laughed in delight. "I tell you, it's a delightful experience – rather like rocking along in a row-boat on a mild swell. Certain I cannot convince you to try it out? We'll be away tomorrow at first light now that you are here and ready for traveling." Ned hesitated, and then blurted, "I'm not really sure of why your fellows are detailed to join us. A Texas Ranger, and a Delaware Indian, with a wet-behind-the-ears ensign and an old soldier like Owen; you must know that my fellows will be curious, having such an odd collection added on to our party at the last minute. We were supposed to test the camels, map out a good alternate road, and hurry along to California… you know, they have found gold there – and in amazing quantities, just this last autumn – and I know about secrecy and the security of missions and all that. I won't ask your purpose in this, but the fellows will wonder. A word to the wise, Jim; have some convincing story to tell in answer to questions. For they will ask them, you know. Around the campfire of an evening."

"Certainly," Jim replied. "Should anyone ask, tell them that we are to recover records and items left in a cache on the banks of the Colorado, after the failure of the O'Neill expedition. The party was sent out at great expense, and following upon the disaster which cost the lives of so many – those records were left concealed for later recovery. Sergeant Owen is our guide in this, as he was one of that party, and Mr. Shaw serves as translator, should we encounter any of the local natives."

Ned Beale nodded, comprehending. "Yes, that is a yarn which will convince. Although there will be embroideries upon it, trust me on that, Jim."

Jim felt a sudden conviction that Ned was far cleverer and more diplomatic than he had let on. Best to change the subject, then. "Gold in California, you say? I had read of it, but thought it was only stories in the sensational press."

"No," Ned shook his head. "'Tis all true about the gold. I brought the samples east myself, not three months ago. It is real and an amazingly rich find; so rich that every fortune-hunter in these States and even farther afield, will be heading California-ward. No, strike that; Captain Reade, I am assured they will be heading to California even as we set out."

"As long as they do not interfere with our mission," Jim insisted, and Ned Beale laughed and clapped him on the shoulder.

Celia Hayes

"Nor mine as well. I tell you, Jim, I do not hunger for riches, myself. Knowledge, experiences, the sight of new horizons... all that is worth more to me than any quantity of gold. Still, 'tis curious. The Spanish came to this place, this new world, avid for gold. And found it, now and again in rich mines and taken from the native tribes in Mexico and Peru. But they never found it here, no matter how their conquistadores searched for the Seven Golden Cities, for Quivera, the greatest of them all. It is a curious coincidence that once their hold on these places in the northern continent was shattered ... that a man building a humble saw-mill should find gold, gold in such quantities to beggar the imagination."

"An irony, indeed." Jim replied. Another thought occurred, as he and Ned watched the camels in their enclosure, walking to and fro with their particular swaying stride. "Ned, what do you think? What do you know of our Sergeant Owen? Is he a man to be trusted?"

"I honestly do not know," Ned replied after a moment of considering silence. "I have heard nothing disparaging to his character. But he is an enlisted man, not an officer. Two worlds, Jim – to us of the profession of arms. I would trust him with my life and the lives of my men, based on his repute. But I do not <u>know</u> him, having never served with him, not as you have with Mr. Shaw." He added, with a smile, "I do not know you, either, save that Colonel Hays, whose reputation as a commander of irregular soldiers is a byword, has vouched for you to the satisfaction of my own commander and to my own."

"Thank you, Ned," Jim replied. "We'll be ready in the morning. Mr. Shaw and I are accustomed to travel light and fast – although I cannot speak for our Army contingent."

158

"They'd better be ready as well," Ned chuckled. "Or they will be playing catch up all the day."

"We'll be ready," Jim said, and strolled away to the ramshackle and rambling quarters – a crude-built dog-trot cabin of logs, from which most of the chinking had already fallen, which the commander at Camp Verde felt to be all the hospitality necessary for visitors, important or not. Toby was already sitting outside of it, cross-legged in Indian fashion, contemplating the fading sunset, a blaze of red, purple and gold on the western horizon.

"We're away in the morning," Jim said, softly. There was a rough bench sitting on the bit of turf outside the cabin. He sank into it. He and Lt. Barnes were bunked for the night in one part of the cabin, Sergeant Owen and Toby in the other – although Toby, as was his usual habit, had taken his bed-roll and spread it out underneath a generously sheltering oak nearby.

"We're away at sunrise," Jim told him, "Camels and all."

"As I expected." Toby nodded and returned to his contemplation of the sunset. Very little surprised Toby. "James, do you think that we will find the missing Captain O'Neill? And that if we do – will he want to return?"

"Of course, we will find him," Jim replied. "We're Jack Hays' finest stiletto-men. And he will wish to return: he is a white man, a soldier. Duty requires it. Why would he not?"

"I have been talking a little with young Barnes," Toby replied. "He said that Captain O'Neill had a ... fondness as a cadet for the tales of Fenimore Cooper, and a great interest in relics and weapons of my people, and those Others. Barnes says that he used to laugh at himself – saying that he was meant to be a wild Indian or an Arab corsair, but by mistake his soul was wrapped in the flesh and bones of a Christian. It struck young Barnes as curious, which is why young he remembered. If such is the case, your Captain may not wish to return, and what would we say to convince him?"

"I don't know," Jim replied. Yes, this was another dimension. "We'll burn that bridge when we get to it, I guess." And yet another random thought occurred to him; his own instinctive dislike of Sergeant Owen. "Toby, do you remember that treacherous Englishman, Vibart-Jones – the one involved in the Wilkinson letters, and the matter of the Spanish treasure at San Saba? I am given to wonder if he has turned up again, in disguise. The man was an actor, after all. And at a squint, Sergeant Owen looks enough like him, and the age is right."

"No, James," Toby shook his head, very definitely. "They are not the same man, even though there is a likeness."

"How can you be so certain?" Jim was diverted, but not convinced. Toby considered gravely, before replying. "Two things, James; things which no man can disguise through art or effort for very long. First, the lobes of Sergeant Owen's ears are not attached to his head, but droop, separately, to the width of my thumb. Vibart the spy – the lobes of his ears were narrow and attached. And have you not noticed how a man favors one hand over the other, for holding a pistol, a knife, a pen? Vibart the English spy favored his left hand. You and I, and Sergeant Owen, all favor our right hand. Sergeant Owen is not Vibart. He is who he claims to be, a soldier of long service in many lands. I would say we can trust him with our lives. Perhaps not with the good name and virtue of our sisters, though." Toby added, with a grin.

***

In the cool of a dew-spangled morning, Ned Beale's exploring party set off; twenty men and a dozen camels, most laden with half a wagon load of gear, and led on a string by Walid Ali and his assistant, the mute Hassim. Jim could not find the proper words to express how very strange and alien they looked; long necks and longer legs, the oddly-humped bodies piled high with gear and supplies, plodding relentlessly along the track from Camp Verde to the north-west.

"They say that every one of them can carry more than four pack mules," Young Joe Barnes observed in admiration. Jim replied, "And smell worse than four pack mules, too." He had already agreed with Ned Beale that he, Toby and the others in their party would ride upwind of the camels on the trail, and picket their horses apart from them at night, although Ned assured him that their horses would eventually become accustomed to the odor and behavior of the beasts. Jim doubted that, profoundly; his own horse – normally a steady-tempered brown gelding turned jittery and restless whenever within sight and smell of the camels, his eyes showing white all the way around. The one pack-mule that he and Toby shared was even more reluctant to associate with the camels. He could only hope that any curious Comanche with a taste for stealing exotic stock would be just as unsettled and their own horses even more so.

Still, the first part of the journey was a relatively pleasant one; folk came out from their houses and fields, just to watch the camels amble past, and to cheer the Federal soldiers in their neat blue uniforms. At long last, perhaps there would be a relief from the dangers of Comanche war parties, striking deep into settled territory! They were invited to settle for the night in pleasant pastures, and more came to marvel at the gangling camels, and to offer hospitality, food, and drink to the soldiers – which was much appreciated. At one camping-place, an obliging Walid Ali clipped a fine harvest of hair from the camels, presenting the women of the locality with better than a bushel of coarse stuff, which they carried away in triumph, saying that they were going to spin it into yarn and knit stockings from it.

What Jim also appreciated – especially when it rained, or an unseasonable spring norther blew – was that among the burdens carried by the camels were several commodious canvas tents. They lived in some comfort, for the soldiers were most practiced at setting up the tents of an evening, and the baggage also included numerous items of folding camp furniture. One soldier in particular proved to be a most accomplished cook, for which all were grateful.

"He was detailed for that skill, let me assure you," Ned Beale asserted. "French creole from New Orleans, prolly got a drop of the African in him, but he looks white enough, and so I don't enquire too close. Best not, when someone is cooking the food you eat. Tastes prime, though, doesn't it?"

"Best Army meal I've ever eaten," Jim acknowledged – for it was. Corporal Fournier was indeed a masterful cook, commander of the cook-fire, the array of skillets and iron ovens deployed over them, the Army rations seasoned with spices and additions conjured up from his own private stores. Even the corporal's corn-dodgers were amazing.

Even better, of an evening after a supper provided by the expert corporal were the yarns told around the fire, for the party proved to have some excellent spinners of same around them. Ned Beale as a raconteur, ordinarily would have been a champion among them, but his stories of California and the fabled gold mines paled next to those told by Sergeant Owen, and most unexpectedly – by Walid Ali. The sergeant had an inexhaustible fund of stories, of his service in India for the British crown and the India Company; accounts of intrigue and spectacle, of Indian princes and princesses, clad in silks and jewels of incredible richness, of deeds of derring-do – most of which Sergeant Owen modestly averred had been those performed by other men, and of which he had only heard second-hand. Walid Ali also had stories; fantastical stories of the middle east, in which names of towns known in the Bible featured heavily; Damascus, Jerusalem, Babylon, and Antioch. Such enthralled the party, every evening, even the mute Hassim, who did not speak but apparently could understand English.

"Poor fellow," Ned explained early on, in answer to Jim and Toby's inquiries. "He's from Baku on the Caspian Sea, so I was told. I'd guess that he is mostly Russian, or Crim Tatar. They say that the local Bey's men cut out his tongue as a punishment for something or other. But he's a hard worker, and does what we tell him. God knows, he could have finished up in worse conditions."

"Curious," Toby remarked, his eyes narrowing thoughtfully. "Now, he is a man who favors his left hand ... I cannot see his ears, though."

They journeyed west into the contested borderlands, and then northerly following the Rio Grande, once past the flowing waters of Comanche Springs – a green oasis in the sere and dusty flatlands. Once or twice they encountered wandering parties of Comanche, but the friendship of Old Owl, Mopechucope of the Penateka still held firm, or so Toby was inclined to remind those who came to parlay and marvel at the camels – doing so from a careful distance. In any case, they were traveling far beyond Comancheria, into the lands traditionally claimed by the western Apache, and those settled tribes, of which Sergeant Owen said planted crops and orchards as fine as any among the whites. There would Jim and Toby complete their mission, for good or ill. The two of them had certainly traveled shorter distances under more perilous and uncomfortable circumstances. But should their mission meet with success – or even if it didn't – they would return to Texas by the same way, although in considerably less comfort, since the camels and the rest of Ned Beale's party intended to carry on all the way into California.

At early summer, they were in the vicinity, so Sergeant Owen said, of that mighty river, a silver thread at the bottom of a cliff-walled red canyon, carved out by eons of floods. Both Ned and Sergeant Owen consulted a set of maps, and made some careful observations with navigational instruments, ultimately announcing that they were within at least a day's journey of the camping-place where the O'Neill expedition had fallen onto disaster.

"We'll know the place," Sergeant Owen announced, magisterially, as they were breaking camp on the following morning, as Walid Ali and Hassim led the camel trail past. Their horses had all become progressively tolerant of the camel presence, although Jim doubted that any of them would ever relish the smell, or the manners of the shambling beasts. "We left a tall cairn of stones marking the graves of our dead in the party."

"And it's such a desolate country, there will not be much that will have overgrown the place in a single season," Ned added. "We are near to the parting of our ways, gentlemen – once you have achieved your mission…"

"I fear so," Jim replied, suddenly diverted by how swiftly the mute Hassim lifted his head at those words, a flash of avid interest in his eyes. A trickle of unease ran down his spine. What did they really know of this mute foreigner, hired in Egypt to mind the camels, or so Ned averred. And Hassim understood English; but exactly how well? Jim's eyes met those of his blood-brother, watchful and wary. Could the English spy possibly have put on the guise of a mute camel-herder from the back of beyond? He was the right age, perhaps, and a left-handed man at that – but the ragged turban and fringe of greying hair hung to his shoulders, veiling his ears.

***

At around noon, they reached the ultimate campsite of the O'Neill party; Jim had to hand it to the perhaps-late Captain O'Neill; he had a fine eye for a place to set up the tents, pasture the beasts of burden and stay for a while. A sheltered pasture of several acres, slightly below the level of the tablelands and sheltered from winds from the north, where the grass grew lush, green, and tall, a dribble of pure clean water from a small tributary-spring which eventually wound its own eccentric way down to the river below – and a few trees, those cottonwoods which set their roots deep wherever there was water. There was even a pleasing view to the north and west, of the river canyon.

"Aye, this is the place," Sergeant Owen said, his voice heavy with the burden of memory. At the edge of the pasture, the cairn of piled river-tumbled stones reminded Jim piercingly of that other cairn; that one in the borderlands, the one with six others, marking the graves of his brother Dan and those of his Rangers, murdered by the traitor Glanton. That had happened not even ten years past. Sometimes it felt to Jim as if it had been an age ago, and sometimes only last week, so immediate was the memory.

He had passed by those six stone cairns by the side of the trail between San Antonio and the borderlands on the Rio Grande several times over those years, and had never failed to add another stone to the one which marked Daniel's grave, a renewal of that promise to his brother; find the traitorous Glanton and see that justice was served. That was where his duty as a Ranger truly began, a duty laid upon him. Likely Sergeant Owen also felt the same never-ending obligation.

Now he said, to Ned and Sergeant Owen, "As agreed, your party stays for about a week, sufficiently long enough for us to venture along the river, toward that Supai town – the one which the missionaries from Mormon territory reported."

"I hope that you may find that person – or, rather that answer which you seek." Ned ventured with commendable discretion. Jim, after consideration and consultation with Toby, Lieutenant Barnes, and Sergeant Owen, had trusted him with the bare bones reason for their search.

***

Ned's party set up camp – tents, portable stove, cook-tent, and all with their usual dispatch, picketing the camels on one side – the down-wind side most distant from camp and the mules and horses on the other. The camels appeared to have inspired only wary curiosity from the Indians and no larcenous intention. Jim had often thought that would have been most amusing. At the best of times, camels were grudgingly cooperative in the skilled hands of Walid and Hassim; in the hands of the most expert thieves of horseflesh on the southern plains? Jim was convinced that the impresario Mr. Barnum could have sold tickets to that comic spectacle. Still, Ned set a regular night guard, as he had all the way along.

"The river is relatively low," Sergeant Owen advised them, after a brief reconnaissance on the day after their arrival. Jim, Toby, and Joe Barnes gathered to hear his report at the edge of camp, well out of earshot. "After the spring floods, an' all. I believe that it will be negotiable with horses and mules, but only lightly packed, and the barest necessities."

"That's how we are accustomed to travel," Jim agreed, recalling how Jack and his brother Daniel had told tales of long days on foot, or on horseback with only ammunition for the weapons and a handful of pecans and jerky for sustenance. "But we have been spoiled by the Army for hard-living."

"Aye, Captain. It's not so much what you have, but what you can do without, cheerfully and in a pinch," Sergeant Owen agreed. "If I recollect, there are many wide places in this canyon which can support a village, with their fields and orchards. I would suggest that we venture along to as many of them as we may. Although it may best serve if Mr. Shaw can ask for a guide from the first and friendliest that we may encounter. Mr. Shaw, I have been assured that you speak many of the native tongues. Are you sure of being understood by the folk we may encounter?"

"I am certain of it," Toby assured him. "I am well-acquainted with the talk of most in this part of the world, and sure of being able to make myself understood. There are always those among a People who are likewise well-traveled."

Joe Barnes had been silent until that point. Now he asked, "For how long will we continue searching? We cannot carry too much in the way of supplies down into the canyon."

"Ned has promised to cache sufficient for our return journey," Jim replied. "I would not hew too narrowly to a time-table, Joe; we need not, if we may trade – we have some small goods, intended as presents – glass beads, metal for arrow-heads, steel needles and such. If spent judiciously, they may supply us for many weeks. It all depends on how soon we find Captain O'Neill, or obtain proof of his fate."

"And you are assured of our safety, in so small a party?" the young lieutenant ventured. "I am not anxious for myself, but with only the four of us…"

Sergeant Owen chuckled. "That may work out to our favor, sir, in that we are clearly no threat and come with friendly intent. If you are bothered about safety, then perhaps the milit'ry and the West are not where to seek it in the first place."

"Fortune favors the bold, Joe," Jim pointed out.

Young Barnes first flushed in chagrin at the implied reproof, then chuckled in a self-deprecating manner. "I trust to the experienced judgment of my seniors," he admitted generously. "And may I suggest that Sergeant Owen and I wear our best dress uniforms when we approach any of the canyon-Indian's villages? It may make a suitably impressive demonstration and if Captain O'Neill is anywhere to be found, perhaps it may recollect his duty to the nation to his memory."

Jim almost replied, *"Don't be ridiculous, lad – this is not a parade through Military Square!"* but he saw that Sergeant Owen was nodding in agreement. Well – the two of them knew Army custom and perhaps the best and subtle way to appeal to O'Neill if he still lived.

"Use your best judgment," he said, although he did have second thoughts, seeing Joe Barnes, resplendent in his fine blue uniform coat, with a red-silk sash fringed with gold under his belt, and a narrow officer's sword hanging from that belt. Sergeant Owen was even more impressive; his upper sleeves barely seen for the stripes of his rank banding them, and a row of decorations on the left breast of his jacket. As they rode away from camp toward the canyon-edge the following morning, Ned Beale grinned and saluted them with a touch of his riding quirt to the brim of his peaked cap, and Walid Ali called, "Sirs, sirs – where are you going in such splendid attire?"

"To retrieve a treasure!" Joe Barnes replied in so transparent a jest that they all laughed – Ned, Jim, Sergeant Owen, and the soldiers watching them depart. Only – and Jim noticed this fleetingly – Walid and Hassim did not. But they were soon over the edge of the canyon and out of sight of all but the canvas tent peaks and the tops of the trees, and very soon not even that.

* * *

Down, down, down that red-walled canyon, impossibly deep – a narrow path, barely wide enough for a horse or mule, twisting and turning – often with a vast drop below his elbow which caused Jim to suck in his breath and not think about how far he and his mount would drop, if the beast missed a step. It was not reassuring, to see birds soaring … down below. Or to see the gravel-strewn and steeply-downward stretches. That poor soldier of O'Neill's exploring party had crawled up the path on hands and knees, which thought did give reassurance to Jim. If a dying man could make it up from river to canyon-edge, then a fit man on a horse could make it down in safety and security to all but his peace of mind. Over some stretches, they did resort to dismounting and leading the animals in single file. Sergeant Owen took the lead, being at least passing-familiar with the path. One stretch, barely wide enough for them to pick their way along, with a sheer drop at their elbow left Jim sweating and feeling rather sick, listening to the silence in which pebbles fell, and then – a very long time later – rattling into the scree and brush at the bottom of that long drop.

Reaching safety at the other end, Sergeant Owen observed jovially, "Cap'n Reade, are y' afraid of heights, then?"

"Not so much a fear of heights, Sergeant," Jim refrained from looking back at the traverse they had crossed. "Only the prospect of falling from them."

"If it's any comfort, sah, this is the worst, or at least it was when I last passed this way."

On down, down again, closer to the thread of river running at the very bottom; now they were in shade, so far had they descended. For many days, the sky had covered them, a blue arching bowl overhead; now the sky seemed flatter, somehow – and at last, when they reached the very bottom, the sky looked small and limited, hung between the cliffs like a stretch of tent canvas. After the dry desert, the air in the deep canyon was moist – one could smell the water, and savor the fresh green scent of growing things.

There was nothing much like a path established at the bottom of the canyon, where the river twisted and rambled around bends, now shallow and chuckling over rocks and shallow rapids, or whispering through stands of reeds. They followed the shoreline, sometimes wading through shallows. The waterfall where O'Neill and his small party had gone over was reduced to a bare trickle, splashing into a pond below with a small misty rainbow shining in the mist. They climbed down cautiously, leading the horses and pack-mule one by one.

"I reckon there are floods through here, often enough," Joe Barnes observed, at a place where the shore was open and wide enough to ride side by side. "I can see there's a few large trees – but mostly small saplings and reeds. It's a pleasant enough oasis, though."

"Oasis it is, in the midst of the American desert," Jim agreed. Ahead of them, Sergeant Owen reined in his horse, and lifted his right hand for attention.

"It's around here – the cave where Mayhew left Captain O'Neill. Our good fortune that the spring thaw is over, and with summer the water is low." He squinted at the sun, now high in the brief patch of sky overhead. "It will get dark early, down here. If I may suggest; we set up camp for the night in late afternoon, before it becomes too dark."

"Agreed," Jim nodded. The Sergeant had proved himself as a good and solid man to reply upon, and Jim regretted his early distrust and suspicions. They carried on, moving at a deliberate pace, expecting to be met around the bend by practically anyone – or anything, and attempting to display a peaceful intent married to an authoritative air of being able to handle any non-peaceful advances to their own advantage.

"It's a pleasant place," Jim ventured to his blood-brother. "Such a place in this country must be well-defended, defended over and above the difficulty of getting down to it. I'd assume that we are being watched."

"You are correct, my brother," Toby's eyes crinkled in amusement. "We have been watched for hours. And even followed. Someone dragged their moccasins on the path that we came down, a while ago. I saw the dust rise in the air at our back-trail. But only briefly."

"Likely a child, or an ambitious young buck, clumsy in a hurry," Jim snorted. "I'd never seen a grown Indian make a mistake like that."

By late afternoon, shadows filled the canyon, although the west-facing eminences were touched the flame, glowing like the embers of a fire. It was a breathtaking sight; yes, this country was arrayed with unexpected marvels, like a plain but clever woman turned out in a splendid gown and a fortune in rich gems. This place was a marvelous scenic jewel, a miracle in the desert, a fortress of solitude guarded by red stone cliffs. No wonder poor Captain O'Neill had become entranced, if the story told by the Mormon missionaries were true.

For that first night, they found shelter in one of those half-caves, scoured out at the foot of a cliff by countless eons of flood currents. The dark fell softly in that place, tempered by the trickle of flowing water. They had a fire burning, from dry wood gathered along the high-water mark; Jim was reminded of that place against a cliff in the Nueces country, where he and Toby first met. Only this camping-place looked out on a slow-moving river, on tall red cliffs lighted with sunset flame, and then turned dark, while the stars prickled the velvet black of the night sky.

"I miss Corporal Fournier's cooking," Joe Barnes remarked. Toby and Sergeant Owen had done the suppertime honors between them; the results being edible and filling, but not a patch on what they had become accustomed to in flavor. "Not that this is unsatisfactory grub; just not as …"

"Tasty," Jim supplied, as both volunteer cooks were admirably pokerfaced at this potential slur against their cooking. "Not to change the subject – but tomorrow morning, we continue along the river-bottom?"

"We do indeed, sah!" Sergeant Owen replied smartly. "For as I do believe, following on another day's journey, this branch of the river will lead us to a wider turning in the canyon and at least one village in it. There may we – that is – Mr. Shaw begin his enquiries properly."

"You think much of the Captain," Jim ventured, idly. "You are so keen to retrieve him."

"Captain O'Neill is a very fine officer," Sergeant Owen's expression was unreadable in the dim firelight under the overhanging mouth of that shallow cave. "It is not my habit, sah, to leave any man behind. It's a matter I am obliged to take personally. Captain O'Neill left me in charge of the party."

"No slight upon you, Sergeant," Jim considered another tin mug of coffee – yes, best, since he was taking the first guard-watch on their tiny camp. "An admirable sentiment, all told. I think that we shall be approached, long before we reach that settlement. You do know that we have been watched, by at least a few pairs of eyes, this day."

"Shockin' lack of preparedness if we had not been," Sergeant Owen nodded. "I observed a blinking flash of light from certain places on the higher cliffs; a sun-flash, I have heard it called. A primitive signaling device. Without a doubt, we are being watched."

"I am certain of it," Toby nodded. "And followed as well."

"Sleep well then, gentlemen," Joe Barnes offered, with an expression of wry cynicism. "I'll take the second watch, Captain Reade."

"Rank has privilege, sah!" Sergeant Owen's stern countenance had almost an expression of humor on it, and they all laughed.

Roused by the birds chirping and rustling the thickets, and the clanking of the coffee pot as Sergeant Owen filled it at the water's edge, Jim woke from a sound and restful sleep. He lay wrapped in his blanket and heavy overcoat, and thought about their mission, and what he knew of Captain O'Neill; fascinated by the trackless West, and the Indian peoples who lived there, a veteran survivor of one of the bloodiest battles in the late war. It might be altogether credible that such a man might prefer to remain here. Which would present a problem for Jim and Toby, if he could not be convinced by Joe Barnes and Sergeant Owen. Yes, a man might have duty to consider, but Jim had no liking for being a jailor, taking a reluctant man back to his comrades. What to do … he drowsed in the warmth of blanket and coat, almost drifting back into sleep.

"The sun is well up, sah," Sergeant Owen reminded him. "And the coffee is strong enough to grow hair on a man's chest if he had no'. We should be on the march very shortly."

"Indeed," Jim accepted an enameled metal Army cup from him with gratitude. "I have long believed that the military might of

Texas and the United States wholly depends on a good supply of coffee."

"I began as a drinker of a fine cup of tea, myself, sah," Sergeant Owen replied. "But have come to a liking for what is the custom of the country. The path of wisdom, they say – in acclimating yourself to reality."

Jim wrapped his fingers around the mug, relishing the warmth and way in which he felt more awake after a couple of sips. Some distance from the fire and out of earshot, Toby squatted on his heels by the waterside, shirtless and splashing himself with handfuls of water scooped from the shallows. Joe Bartlett was also preparing for the day, likewise shirtless, but armed with a straight razor and a small mirror, shaving himself with brisk efficiency.

"Are we still being followed, do you think?" Jim asked. Sergeant Owen was already arrayed in the martial splendor of the previous day, precise, correct and every button polished.

"Depend on it, sah," he replied, not sounding in the least worried. "Likely watching us this very minute. Just to be certain of our intentions. Nothing to concern yourself with."

"Sergeant," Jim ventured; his renewed apprehension about Captain O'Neill were troubling. "I have thought again of what I know of the man we are searching for. Should we find him alive and well, will he be willing to return with us? I have begun to wonder, considering what I have been told of him, and what I see of this place…"

"If he is alive and in his right mind, he will come along like a good lad," Sergeant Owen flicked an invisible speck of ash off his immaculate coat. "Of that I am as certain as I am of anything."

"How can you be so certain?" Jim asked, and was utterly rocked at Sergeant Owen's reply. "Because he is my nephew, sah." Sergeant Owen glanced at the other two of their party, still at their brief bath and preparation for the day's march. "I say this in confidence, o'course. No one else should know, y'see. Because he is an officer, commissioned by an act of Congress. Perhaps things are looser in these United States than what I am accustomed to, sah. I will not deny it but there is still the distance, you see. Necessary it is, because of the proper way of things. Captain O'Neill, he is the son of my only sister Emily, who married an Irishman; he had a trade, y'see. An ambitious man. He wished to emigrate some fifteen years ago, it was. He did well for himself – but they are both dead of the yellow fever, now, to my great grief. Emily – she always looked to me, and Patrick O'Neill was a fine and decent man for all that. Hardworking, never treated her ill, and she was my little sister. My only kin, you will understand. And Brendan – such a brave little tyke! He looked up to me, all in my scarlet regimentals, and wished to be a soldier, too. Ye must know how children can be so adoring. Wouldn't be turned aside from that; not him, not ever. Even when Patrick and Emily chose to take Brendan and the other children to Philadelphia – they wrote to me of this, since I was far away in India. At that time, I was done with my last enlistment with John Company – so why not seek another horizon? I did so …"

Sergeant Owen heaved up a great sigh, from the core of his being. "And – well, I had no other trade, y'see, and too old to start learning another. I was good at being a soldier. And a barracks was where I was at home … all the life that I have ever known; bugles and drums and turn out for parade, see to what needed doing, ever since I took the shilling when I was a mere lad of fifteen. Value that had; to the federal Army! So I 'listed again, and for my soldiering prowess, I climbed up the ranks, yet again. Then Brendan was given a place at West Point – to become an officer! Ye can hardly credit it, but Emily came to me, all in tears when the war with Mexico began. I was at the garrison at Carlisle Barracks then, training cavalry soldiers for service on the frontier. Look after him, keep him safe, she begged me; He's going to the war. D'ye have sisters, sah? Sisters whom ye can remember on leading-strings? Holding them in your arms, chasing away a barking dog, and telling them stories about how y'll always keep them safe?"

"I have sisters," Jim confessed. "And they are close to my age but I could not resist such an appeal, since I love them very dearly. What did you do, then?"

"I could not go with him to Mexico," Sergeant Owen answered sadly. "My value was too great to my own company. But I was there, when he returned. It would break your heart, so see him so pale and reduced. Poor Emily was certain he was sickening with the consumption. He fought like a tiger, y'see; when he was taken captive at Monterray and was wounded again in the fighting after he escaped. I did what I could. It is in my mind, sah, as the hero of the moment, Brendan pulled strings of his own, to get me assigned to his expedition into the Colorado country. Never mind that. Once done, I could tell Emily that I would protect him as best that I could, wi' out anyone being t' wiser…"

"Promises," Jim mused. "Promises to kin – they weigh on us all. Even those spoken privately to the dead, with none to witness. And what happened then?"

"It went very well," Sergeant Owen's decorated chest expanded with pride. "I have said before – he was a fine officer, had the right touch. He would leave me to handle the enlisted men, the basics of the expedition. We worked together, settling everything to do with the expedition in a quiet and orderly manner. He took my advice in a considerate fashion, respecting my experience…"

"Considerable experience," Jim conceded generously. "As the general said, likely you have forgotten more than many others have ever learned."

Sergeant Owen nodded, in honest acceptance of the compliment. "Aye, so. I did not worry overmuch when he set off to explore the river in the boat; there was no earthly way that I could go with him, not given my authority over the party. I thought that little could go wrong…"

"Until it did," Jim hoped that he sounded more confident than he felt. "A thing that one cannot foresee. When we come to the first village, let Mr. Shaw take the lead. If your nephew is above ground, I am certain that we shall find him, and convince him to return."

***

They set off, threading their way between the towering red walls of the canyon as it turned and twisted, the sky above that jagged silhouette as blue as the turquoise stones with the Indians of those parts treasured. The watercourse flowed clear as crystal, splashing and chuckling to itself, now and again cascading in a lacy white froth over a low fall and into a deeper pool, of a blue that rivaled the color of the sky. All the canyon bottom was green with new growth, alive with the sounds of birds. A turtle basking on a sun-bleached log vacated that place, plopping clumsily into the water. A spiny cactus anchored to a rocky outcrop above their heads sported a garland of bright red blooms.

"We're still being watched, I take it?" Jim ventured, low-voiced to Toby, who nodded absently, his gaze momentarily over his shoulder on the canyon walls behind them. They were riding ahead of Joe and Sergeant Owen, out of earshot and consulting in low voices.

"Yes... and followed as well. Someone who is ... trail-wise but clumsy; not one of the Blue-Green Water People whose' home this is. Or even one of the Hopituh – the Peaceful Ones. I would not even see any hint of them, if it were. A *Shëwanahkòk*, a man of your people, I think."

"Did one of Beale's party follow us?" Jim asked, and his blood-brother shrugged in his usual inscrutable manner.

"I think it must be so. They are the only *Shëwanahkòk* that we know of. Unless it is a renegade, long accustomed to the wilderness. Such a one to make a way out here – would be most unlikely."

Jim mentally reviewed those of Beale's men; he couldn't think of any among them who had unexpected talents and a willingness to venture alone into the desert wilderness. They were Army troopers; cavalrymen the most of them. Some were veterans of the war in Mexico, but the larger part were barely-trained recruits, albeit with a sense of curiosity and adventure. There were no seasoned frontiersmen among them that he could recall.

"We'll burn that bridge when we come to it," he decided, finally, at which Toby grinned. "As we always do, Brother. I smell wood-smoke and cookfires; we are not very far from the village."

Jim nodded, in complete agreement. "It was supposed to be in a wide place, where several canyons came together ... where the Blue-Green Water People were accustomed to plant and tend their crops during the summer … well, prepare yourself for a grand entrance. Here is where we begin our mission of diplomacy."

"Ready, willing and able, sah!" Sergeant Owen, near enough to overhear this last exchanged, straightened his shoulders. "Leff-tenant – you should do the honors, and ride out in the lead."

"An officer's duty," Joe Barnes grinned, "To go in front and be shot at first, eh?"

"It's why you have the fancy uniform, and get paid so generously," Jim added, and Joe grinned even more widely.

They advanced cautiously around the next few bends in a canyon which widened gradually as they advanced, Joe Barnes in the lead, with a slender and straight length of green sapling resting like a spear on his booted foot. One of his own clean white handkerchiefs was fastened to the other end; "A flag of truce shouldn't go amiss," he suggested. "To make clear our peaceful intent."

It seemed to Jim to be as sensible a suggestion as any other, although he was inwardly thanking his Maker that the Blue-Green Water People were nothing like as warlike as the Comanche – which if they had been, there would have been no visiting Mormon missionaries … or at any rate, not for very long. And there would have been no reason to search for a missing US Army officer, either – save for giving what was left of his corpse a decent burial.

The canyon widened, as they saw when they came around the final bend; widened to encompass a space as flat as a ballroom floor, and green … green with crops of corn, melons and beans, interspersed with scattered trees and the kind of brush arbor dwellings that Toby said were called wickiups, as far as the eye could see within the confines of sheer red crags. There were people moving in the fields, weeding or watering, or busying themselves in the shade; women grinding corn, or weaving baskets, a handful of small children playing a game which seemed to involve much shouting and chasing each other. It all presented a scene of quiet domesticity. To Jim's mild chagrin, there seemed only a mild degree of interest in their arrival, although one woman straightened from her cook-fire, and pointed them out to a man industriously fletching arrows in the shade of a spindly tree. Only the children had anything like active curiosity about the strangers; they abandoned their game and approached with wary interest.

Toby slid from his horse, and walked beside Joe Barnes, holding up his free hand in a gesture intended to show that he was not armed. He called to the children; it sounded like a question. They replied in chorus, like excited birds, and like birds, scattered, all but one older girl, about ten years old, who hung back and watched them with lively interest. Toby spoke over his shoulder, "I have asked to speak to the chief men among them … and asked if there were any of your people living here among them. I said also that we came in peace, with no hostile intent."

"What did they say?" Jim asked, and Toby shrugged.

"They are fetching those who are the heads of families among them – the elders. They will come to us under the shade of that tall tree. But the children did say there was a man of our people living among them. They spoke of it as if there was no great secret,"

"Could it be Captain O'Neill?" Jim looked around at the village, peaceful under the midday sun, lush and green with growing crops, and woven through with the sound of water.

"The children say that he is very lame, walks with a crutch, and has a scar on his cheek that is shaped like that cliff-edge, up there." Toby pointed to a jagged tower of rock, far above, on the lip of the canyon.

"Captain O'Neill has – had just such a scar," Sergeant Owen nodded. "What else did the children tell you, Mr. Shaw?"

"They like him very much, although they think that he is a little mad ... for he is building a waterway, to bring water to the planted crops through a ditch. Very silly, they think. What can be better than how they have always carried water to the plants?"

"You'd be surprised," Jim recollected how the old Spanish friars had built the network of channels – the acequias, to bring water from the springs around San Antonio to the crops they planted. *Could it be that this was what O'Neill was trying to do here? And for what?* "We'll wait for the chiefs and elders under that far tree, and consult with them over this matter. Since the man that we seek appears to be accepted as one of their People, whether it be through losing his memory or by his own free will."

"Well-considered, my brother," Toby murmured, and Jim murmured in reply, "Well, it is always considered tactful to consult those who believe they are in charge ... regardless of what we may say, or do at a later date."

They led their horses to the tallest tree, a monumental cottonwood tree veiled in a cloud of trembling green leaves, somewhat to the center of what seemed to be the Blue-Green Water People's village. They were led there by the older girl, who chattered to Toby in her language, skipping and dancing ahead of them along the well-trodden and dusty track

"She is a Younger Daughter," Toby explained, in between lively conversation with her. "Her Older Sister is the one who took on the main duty of caring for the crippled stranger. He lives in the lodge of their father, who has no living sons. He looks upon the Crippled One as a potential son. He doesn't think that the Crippled One will ever amount to much, being a cripple – but Older Sister is fond of him, and now he can speak their language and do work in their plantings, even wield a spear and bow without entirely disgracing himself. Younger Daughter likes him – she finds him amusing. She is the one who has been teaching him the language of the Blue-Green Water People over the last year, since they found him dying in a cave up-stream. And if he gives Older Sister strong and able sons, then he will be of worth to the People." With a sideways glance at Jim, Toby added. "The People think in long terms, Brother."

"As do ours," Jim replied. They had arrived at the tall poplar tree in the midst of the village. "If he knows that ours want him back – will he willingly return?"

"I cannot say," Toby returned. There was no one waiting yet under the trembling green leaves of the large poplar. Without conversation, he and Toby unharnessed their horses, and spread out several of the thick blankets on the ground underneath of it. They settled onto the blankets, Joe and Sergeant Owen somewhat awkwardly on Jim's urging.

Within the space of a dozen leisurely minutes, the elders of the village converged upon the tall cottonwood tree; a dozen stocky and amiable-appearing men, called from whatever business they were doing in the middle of the day. Jim liked what he had seen of the Blue-Green Water People so far. They seemed to be close kin in attitudes to Toby's Delaware tribe. A people of open mind and toleration, living for their farms and crops, as different from the warlike and slave-trading Comanche as a tame dog to a wild wolf of a wilderness pack.

"They ask for what purpose we have come to this village," Toby reported. "And I have explained about Captain O'Neill; that he is one of our people, a notable chief and much respected. They asked why we did not come searching for him earlier, and I explained that all thought him dead and beyond all aid."

"What are they saying in return?" Joe fiddled with the fringes of his sash. "Do they not believe us?"

"They do, I think," Toby replied. "But is of little moment to them. The Crippled One is his own man, and yet accepted among the Blue-Green Water People. If he remains with them, or returns to his own, that is a choice of his own making. They will neither force him to stay or expel him from their village … although I think the father of Older Sister and Younger Daughter would prefer him to remain. That is the elder, wearing necklace of blue stone in the style of the Hopituh."

The gentleman in question was stocky man, grizzled with middle-age, who chose to remain standing, leaning against the tree; he was the one they had first seen, fletching arrows. An unstrung bow was slung over his shoulder. His eyes appeared keen, the eyes of a good hunter, although he did seem mildly exasperated with Younger Daughter, which was still chattering away nine to the dozen at his side, completely innocent of the concept of elders of the tribe conferring with the strangers. An indulgent parent, Jim surmised.

"They say that we have leave to speak with the Crippled One," Toby relayed, "Although they would not have denied us such – unless he had refused outright to parlay with us. He is across the stream, working at the upper waters. They think he is a fool, but are indulgent of his preoccupation. The girl, Younger Daughter, will show us the path."

They set off again on foot again, leaving the horses ground-staked to the patch of shade of the towering cottonwood tree, following the girl along one of those other winding paths among the fields and crops planted by the Blue-Green Water People.

"It is a comfortable and peaceful prospect," Joe remarked. "And I can see why this would appeal to the O'Neill that I knew. He so loved the tales of Cooper, and the brave Mohicans! And of course, this settlement must be so prosperous that I am certain they would need warriors to defend it in this barren wasteland."

"That is a certainty," Toby replied. "And the Blue-Green Water People are resolute. Which is why they maintain their settlement and fields here. Did you not see their bows and arms? This is their place, their fortress, and they have held it for moons uncounted against those who would take it ... or take the harvest of their fields from them."

"Ah," Joe replied, with a wry expression. "I see. Constant vigilance and the practice of the warlike arts is the natural price paid for freedom from starvation and slavery? That should not surprise me, Mr. Shaw. That was one of the tenents taught to us with much pain at the Academy. It does not surprise me," he added, as the path took a particularly tangled stretch through a thicket of native willow and reeds at the head of another creek emptying into the main watercourse. Now they began seeing that there was another watercourse, a dry and man-made one, narrow and made of carefully fitted flat stones, made waterproof with lime plaster. Jim's eyebrows lifted – lime plaster, here among the Indians? This looked to be a very well-thought-out design; the students at West Point trained as engineers, and this was worthy of an ancient Roman waterworks, such as could be done by a single man, working alone. Around and up a narrow footpath past a chuckling waterfall, until the canyon opened out again, this time into a smaller meadow. The stream widened into a deep still pool in the center of the meadow. There was a small brush arbor here, a heavy blanket of Indian weave spread in the shade before it, and a pile of squared stones near the water's edge. A single human figure straightened from his labors, digging out a trench leading to the pool and shaded his eyes to look at the oddly-assorted party approaching. Younger Daughter ran to him and embraced him in happy exuberance, chattering all the while; a tall scar-faced white man, with light hair straggling to his shoulders, dressed in Indian leggings and a long calico shirt. He set down the shovel and took up a crude crutch, and limped to meet them, his face completely impassive, quite unsurprised. The men all looked silently at each other for a long moment before Jim spoke.

"Captain O'Neill, I presume," Jim turned over several possible greetings in his mind as they walked up the path from the village. "Reade, of the Texas Rangers. We were sent to find you." No presumption – there was the jagged white scar across his face.

Joe spoke almost at the same time. "O'Neill, my god – everyone thought you were dead."

"Brendan, lad, we've come to take you home." That was Sergeant Owen, plainly moved and forgetting that no one was supposed to know of their kinship.

Brendan O'Neill wiped the sweat off his face with the back of his hand, and leaned more heavily on his crutch. He spoke softly to Younger Daughter in the language of the Blue-Green Water folk, and she ran off to search among the tall reeds at the far edge of the pond, leaving the five men to their parlay. "Uncle Owen ... you might find it hard to credit, but I am already home. Here, among the People who have taken me in."

"You can't mean that," Joe protested, and O'Neill's expression turned even grimmer, as if haunted by demons and ghosts. He looked like a man half-in the grave, tired, gray-faced and worn to a thread by whatever had driven him to the wilderness and bidden him to stay. "What about your parents, your friends ... and Rebecca! Did you have no thought for them, at all?"

"I did," O'Neill replied, "And then I didn't. I don't want any of it, any more. Ma and Pa have other sons, Rebecca will find other suitors, if she has not already. I'm done with it all."

"Those are harsh words, Brendan, lad." Sergeant Owen spoke softly, "My sister and your father grieved for you, lad – grieved until they were taken from us, this last winter. They cared for you, and would have rejoiced to know that you lived after all."

"I ... I'm sorry for the grief that I have caused them," Brendan O'Neill replied. His shoulders slumped, as the implication of Sergeant Owen's words sank in. "I am ... sorry at this news. But it's hard to explain ... how everything was different after Mexico. After Monterray."

"You're an officer, O'Neill!" Joe Barnett could hardly contain himself. "You wore this uniform, fought for it – swore an oath to the Army – how could you consider walking away from all that! What kind of man are you, then?"

"What kind of man?" O'Neill looked even wearier. "Well, then I will tell you. I beg of you to allow me to sit down for a while. The leg pains me very much, still. It has never healed satisfactorily."

He led them limping, to the brush arbor, with Sergeant Owen hovering like an attentive nurse over a sick child.

Joe and Jim walked a little behind, Joe saying in an undertone, "He is much changed – I can hardly believe such a change in a man were possible."

"Oh, indeed," Jim answered, suddenly feeling a lifetime older than Joe. "There are many such – having seen the elephant, they have never been quite the same again. I have seen it myself of such friends who saw hard fighting in the war, saw their friends killed before their eyes, or mortally wounded, to sit by them as they died. I am not even the same man as I was in the aftermath of the Salido Creek fight, when I was first sworn in as a Ranger – although my own service was of … was of a different nature."

Sergeant Owens and his nephew were already talking when Joe and Jim joined them, Toby sitting cross-legged, Indian fashion close by.

"They are close kin?" Joe marveled. "I should have known – they look so much alike, and I never saw it, like a fool! And here I have been traveling with Sergeant Owens for these many months past!"

"You looked at the uniform, not at the man," Jim replied, with the weary feeling that he was explaining to an innocent no older than Younger Daughter. "A good enough reason for the Rangers to not wear them – although I understand that experiment was made … once."

"Didn't take, this experiment?" Joe grinned, mischievously and Jim grinned in reply. "I wasn't there when it was tried, but I know men who were. Never again; Jack – Colonel Hays – had the sense never to try it during the war, no matter how often we were made mock of by Yankee cartoonists."

"Still," Joe added, his voice just above a whisper. "Why would he choose this humble life, over and above the other – family, glory, position and advantages?"

"Because sometimes they do not matter," Jim replied, thinking again of how many of his missions for the Rangers would be buried – as Jack had pointed out – in government files, buried away in archives. No, he and Toby were not in it for glory or renown; only for the quiet aid rendered to the helpless, the sinned-against, and those unjustly-condemned. "Shush – listen, he is talking."

"… I began to think that my life was a fraud," O'Neill was saying to his uncle as Jim and Joe approached. "Everything about it, Uncle. Even before I finished at the Academy, I had my doubts … but you see, everyone and everything about my life was telling me in solo and chorus that it was what I was told. What I was told to be; everyone's pride, the gallant son and soldier. I wanted to be like you, Uncle Owen – and for a long while, I could pretend to be, while everyone said how proper and honorable and good it was. But I couldn't – not really. I was broken at Monterray, although no one ever suspected. I came to think that I hated the whole imposture. And then – to come back from that, and pretend to be the beau ideal of society…" Now Brendon O'Neill looked even more desperate. "I was a fraud, Uncle, and knew it, I just knew that everyone could see it about me; that I was a cowardly fraud dressed up in a fancy uniform. I could think of nothing but getting away. Command of an exploring party into the far West territories was the perfect solution. And then ..."

"The boat, and carried away in the flood," Sergeant Owen nodded. Quietly, Jim and Joe joined them under the shade of the arbor, while O'Neill continued.

"It was, I think – like dying in a nightmare and awakening to life – into another life, a simpler one. They say that I was raving for many days and weeks. At first, I couldn't really remember who I was, what I was doing in a brush wickiup. Not that I minded. It seemed as if I was living in a dream come to real life. And when I recalled my own life before, and compared it to here, I did not want to return to it. This suits me better. And since my parents are dead, that only leaves Becky. I ... we had words before I departed for the West, so I am not at all certain that our promise to wed holds."

"She carried on as if you were her perfect gentle knight," Joe spoke for almost the first time to O'Neill. "And pestered her father to move heaven and earth to return you to her."

O'Neill chuckled, a short and humorless bark of laughter. "Oh, I am certain that it was Becky's vanity that led her to that, rather than affection for me."

"I am certain that Miss Bartlett's affections were true and honorable," Joe sounded indignant on her behalf, and O'Neill chuckled again, sounding weary rather than humorless. "She loved the picture of me as portrayed in the penny press, not the man that I am. She's a pretty child in love with a fairy-tale hero, Joe. I know that very well. I daresay she feels guilty for her words to me when I refused to give up the notion of the expedition. She will get over the loss of a fiancée, if she has not done so already. When you return

East, Joe, tell her I am dead and buried. She will cry pretty tears, dab them away with a lace handkerchief, and look around for another susceptible male heart. I will pray that she lands upon yours, after all."

"You dispose of Miss Bartlett as if she were a mere bauble," Joe's blue-coated back was rigid with disapproval, even sitting on the ground under the arbor. O'Neill sighed again.

"A bauble that I have no real estimation for, Joe. But believe me – I wish her the best, knowing full well that I am not the man for her, and perhaps never had been. You ..."

A small cry broke into their converse, a cry from the small Indian girl, Younger Daughter, and they all looked up, startled. Toby sprang to his feet, the trusty club in hand and knife in the other, but to no avail, for the man who held her by her hands behind her back and a knife at her throat stood not twenty feet from them – a broad-shouldered man, at once horribly familiar in several ways: Hassim the mute camel-herder, who had shed his robe and turban for the nondescript trousers, boots, and a round jacket worn by civilized folk. But it appeared that he was not mute, after all – and the tenor of that voice sent a chill down Jim's back, even as he reached for the trusty Colt at his side.

"You! Tell me where you have hidden the treasure, or the girl dies! I swear to you – she dies, unless you show me, now! Not a move from you, Reade – the brat dies and it will be on you!"

Vibart-Jones, the English spy and treasure-hunter. No wonder that Jim's memory and Toby's suspicions had been sparked; although diverted by Vibart-Jones' untoward guise. What had the man been doing, hired in foreign parts as a lowly camel-drover, pretending to be mute? With a small part of his mind, Jim thought it likely that the English spy was bent on the US Army's camel experiment. Such a venture would be of interest to a great power, a power which had an envious eye on the American continent and a means of expanding their influence on it.

"There is no treasure here," O'Neill gasped, as he struggled to his feet, with his crutch. "Only the treasure of simple lives…"

"You lying bastard," Vibart-Jones snarled, as he pressed the knife-blade closer on Younger Daughter's small throat. "I know who you are – and you too, Reade. Come not a step closer! Where is it?"

"What?" Jim kept his voice level and detached with an effort. "There is no treasure concealed here, or anywhere else. Ned spoke in jest, as we departed from his party. The San Saba silver is long gone, Jones; gone to assuage the suffering of poor folk, all throughout Texas and Mexico. I do not have it, or know the details of where it has gone. Are you planning to go and rob every church, convent or orphanage?"

"Shut you! And raise your hands so that I can see them!" Vibart-Jones snapped, and Jim quailed to see a small thread of blood trickle down Younger Daughter's throat. But the child was a stoic; only her eyes pleaded with them – and especially with O'Neill.

"You are an English gentleman," Jim began, thinking to appeal to the man's better nature, if he indeed possessed such, but at that moment there was a near-silent harp-note of a bow-string drawn and released, and the crash of a Colt. In the same instant that the arrow flew, Sergeant Owens had snatched Jim's Colt from the holster on his hip and fired a shot, a shot which splashed a cicatrice of red on the English spy's forehead. A very fine shot with a weapon new to him, Jim thought in a distracted moment – but of course, a soldier of such long service would be. Perhaps he should ask Sergeant Owen for tutoring in marksmanship.

Vibart-Jones crumpled like a sack of dirty clothes, as the father of Younger Daughter rose from the brief concealment at the edge of the still, deep pool which would supply O'Neill's waterworks. Younger Daughter fled to his embrace, now sobbing like an ordinary child, and for a moment, that was the only sound in the little valley, save for the cries of affronted birds.

"Who the hell was that man?" O'Neill leaned on his crutch, gasping with the effort, even more gray in the face than before.

"A spy, murderer and torturer," Jim replied. "And a foreigner to boot. It doesn't matter. He never found what he came here for, anyway."

Sergeant Owen ceremonially handed Jim's Colt to him, saying, "Thank ye, sah, for the loan of this – sorry, I did no' have the time to ask permission."

"Think nothing of it, Sergeant," Jim replied. "Only one shot – most excellent. Better to ask for forgiveness afterwards than permission too late. Having resolved the question of who was following us, down the canyon, we should resolve the question of what to do regarding our mission regarding Captain O'Neill."

His gaze went to O'Neill, and Younger Daughter, who now was leaning against him, her arms about his waist and crying like a normal child, while her father stood close to them both. He did not have another arrow nocked, which Jim took as a good thing.

Sergeant Owen fetched up a deep sigh, from the bottom of his soul, as it sounded. "We have found no one here," he intoned. "Save a man of the Blue-Green Water People. And an English spy, who shall go unlamented into a grave. Do ye agree, Captain Reade, and so shall ye swear?"

"I will," Jim replied, and Toby nodded in silent agreement, as did Joe, after a small hesitation. "There is no one here but a man of the Blue-Green Water tribe, who, having made a choice, shall live with it to the end of his days."

Over Younger Daughter's head, O'Neill nodded gratefully.

***

"I hope that his water-channeling scheme will work out," Joe Barnes remarked, as they rode away, back up through that deep canyon. "And … say this to no one, Captain Reade – but I hope that Captain O'Neill will be happy in his choice of life."

"There is no Captain O'Neill," Jim replied. "Only a man of the Blue-Green Water People. Remember that, Joe. Only that."

Into the Wilds

Notes – Lone Star Sons

The First Adventure

As in the first set of adventures, this is still a work of fiction. Like the first adventure in *Lone Star Sons*, this adventure draws on the aftermath of General Adrian Woll's brief takeover of San Antonio in the spring of 1842. The re-occupation of San Antonio lasted only a week or so, but the district court had been meeting, and fifty-five Anglo-Texian men – court officials, litigants and witnesses were taken as prisoners of war. Jim Reade's father was one of this number taken prisoner and eventually deposited in Perote Prison at hard labor.

To the men taken into Mexico by Woll's army were added a handful of survivors of the Dawson Massacre on the banks of Salado Creek. A party of Texian militia from Bastrop lead by Nicholas Mosby Dawson arrived too late to join the main force of Texians setting up an ambush on the main Mexican force were isolated and wiped out by Woll's retreating rear guard. Fifteen survivors of Dawson's company were taken along with the San Antonio prisoners. A punitive expedition followed after Woll's prudently retreating army, led by Alexander Somervell, who went no farther than Laredo before declaring that honor had been satisfied and that his army of volunteers and Texas Rangers could therefore decamp for home.

But a number of his volunteers voted to continue on over the border, elected another commander and carried on. They took the town of Mier, but were forced to surrender when Mexican forces counterattacked. Now another large party of Texians were headed toward durance vile in Perote Prison, marched by slow stages – west to Monterray and Saltillo, and then south, deeper into the interior.

Just short of Saltillo, two hundred of them overpowered their guards and fled north into the desert. Having no food and little water with them, they were all easily recaptured, clapped into leg-irons and taken to Saltillo. His Excellency Santa Anna was infuriated by this, and ordered all recaptured prisoners to be executed. International outrage from the American and British foreign ministers forced Santa Anna to dial back and settle for simple decimation instead: only one in ten would be executed. Seventeen black beans and 159 white beans were placed in a pottery jar and covered with a light cloth. The prisoners were made to reach into the jar and draw a bean. Those who drew a black bean were separated from the others, given a last meal, last rites from a priest if they wished it, blindfolded, and executed in two groups; the infamous "Black Bean Draw." A rumor that Jeremiah Nichols had drawn a black bean had the repercussions outlined in this first adventure.

The Second Adventure

While there are plenty of folk tales of creatures like the 'chupacabra' extant in the borderlands along the Rio Grande, this "Beast" is entirely made up by me. My daughter had been reading a book about a real-life series of killings in 18th-century France by the "Beast of Gévaudan" – which may have been one or more monstrous wolves, wolf-dog hybrids, or something even more ferocious and exotic – a matter which still puzzles the experts. It is estimated that nearly a hundred men, women and children were attacked by the

Beast, or series of beasts, many of them children or young teenagers out with flocks of cattle, sheep or goats in a particularly wild and mountainous part of south-central France. The existence and murderous onslaught of the "Beast of Gévaudan" excited the interest of Louis XV, who offered rewards and encouraged professional hunters to bag the "Beast" and put an end to the slaughter of his rural subjects.

It was my own inspiration to make the Texian "Beast" into a chimpanzee, after reading certain recent news accounts of attacks by full-grown male chimpanzees on humans. No one on the 19th century north American frontier would have been baffled in the least discovering the bloody aftermath of attacks by known animals, like a wolf, bear, or mountain lion on a human being, but a chimpanzee would have been something rarely seen save perhaps in book illustrations. A full-grown male chimpanzee can be as much as 200 pounds and is four times stronger than a human male – and the damage that they can inflicted on a human is terrible to contemplate.

The Third Adventure

This adventure and characters are all imaginary. It was inspired by a suggestion from a reader of *Lone Star Sons*, involving a 19th century murder case of a man who pled self-defense in the murder of his wife, by claiming she had shot at him first, and by way of proof, showing a bullet-hole in the shirt which he had been wearing. It was not until someone took a second and much-magnified look at the so-called bullet-hole, that they realized that the fabric around the edge of that hole should have been slightly scorched by the passage of a white-hot bullet. That sudden enlightenment led to a murder conviction against the husband.

In this version, I included the element of a serial-killer husband, which is from my imagination. However, for much of the 19th century, or even earlier, it was not unheard of for husbands to desert wives, and vice versa. In a day when few traveled beyond twenty or thirty miles from wherever was home or where people knew your face, it would be quite a simple matter to relocate to a different city, or another state and take on a new identity. Calling yourself by a new name or claiming to be single or a widow/widower was the practical method of do-it-yourself divorce in that day. It was not until photographic images became common, and the regular practice of law enforcement to distribute them widely that taking on a new identity became any more complicated than moving a hundred miles away.

The Fourth Adventure

In all but one aspect, this adventure is an exaggeration of what went on when the *Mainzer Adelsverein* – the Society of Gentlemen of Bibrach-am-Mainz – was doing a preliminary investigation of the possibilities of taking up an entrepreneur grand in Texas. There were several members of the consortium of nobles hoping to make good and do good out of filling a tract of Texas land with good German farmers, craftsmen and technicians who made exploratory trips to the Wild (Texas) frontier – although on behalf of the *Adelsverein*, rather than specifically for Prince Frederick William of Prussia. The three gentlemen of science are entirely fictional, although Professor Kraus is loosely based on the geologist and naturalist Ferdinand Von

Roemer, who made an extensive study of the geology of Texas during a long excursion in 1845-46. The incident of Herr Doktor Maier performing cataract surgery on a Comanche warrior is based on a true historical incident; the operation was performed by Doctor Ferdinand Ludwig von Herff, who came to Texas in 1847 as part of a circle of young men called the "Forty", with plans to establish an idealistic utopian commune along ideas fashionable at the time. Herff and his friends brought along everything they would need – including a woman housekeeper and all of Dr. Herff's medical gear. They established their commune near present-day Castell. It didn't last a year, but that was where the cataract operation was successfully performed and the satisfied patient rewarded his doctor with a girl. Lena, or Lina was her name; she had been a captive for a long time and never able to recall enough about her original family to return to them. Eventually, she married one of Dr. Herff's friends among the "Forty." Dr. Herff himself practiced medicine tirelessly for most of the next sixty years, establishing San Antonio's first hospital, several medical associations, serving on the Texas Board of Medical Examiners, and founding the town of Boerne.

The Fifth Adventure

The basic premise of this adventure is taken from a novel which was made into a visually-fascinating move; *Dances With Wolves*. Beautiful movie, stuffed with scenic panoramic sweeps of the Northern Plains, attractive and interesting actors, especially those portraying Sioux. There is no better means for getting an idea of what a Sioux village and inhabitants looked like in the mid-19th century, short of a living history exhibit. Everything else about *Dances* fell apart for me after that. What was the purpose of a small Army post abandoned out in the middle of the plains? US Army forts were established along the overland trail to protect commercial and emigrant traffic. An army post just sitting out there with no mission, off and away off the beaten track is a logical fail for me. Another logical fail was that by the 1860s, it just wasn't historically credible for an Army officer to 'go native' and join an Indian tribe. This did happen fairly often at an earlier point in the history of the American frontier, depending on the tribe and the eccentricity of the individual. The early mountain men cheerfully and openly joined various friendly tribes, and other men whose work or wanderlust led them into the trans-Mississippi West during the 1830s and 1840s were candidates for adoption as adults into a tribe. This final adventure is my attempt to 'fix' these inconsistencies, make the hero a traumatized survivor of the Mexican-American War, move the story back in back in time almost fifteen years, another location, and give him an assignment to survey a portion of land which the Americans had won from Mexico. *(There were many surveying and exploring missions going on at that time.)* Get him separated from the rest of his group, and stranded in the wilderness … and play out the rest of it as I have outlined in this story.

I did tweak other circumstances chronologically, though; those to do with the US Army Camel Corps, which was not activated and set up at Camp Verde in Texas until several years after the year in which this story was set. The explorer, Lt. Edward "Ned" Beale who features in this story, was a real person, and quite famous in his day; sailor, soldier, war hero, explorer, spy, diplomat, man about town, and confidant of presidents … as well as being a champion of the use of camels in exploring those stretches of the south-west won by the United States in the Mexican-American War.

Celia Hayes

www.ingramcontent.com/pod-product-compliance
Lightning Source LLC
Chambersburg PA
CBHW031418250626
47155CB00004B/1543